BUSTING OUT
By Diane Kelly

Cover Design by Lyndsey L.

Copyright © 2020 Diane Kelly
All Rights Reserved

Acknowledgements

I have lots of people to thank for making this book happen. Many thanks to Colene Drace (pictured below) for teaching me about the biker life, especially from a woman's perspective. Thanks to my editor Holly Ingraham for your helpful feedback. Thanks to cover artist Lyndsey Lewellen of Lewellen Designs for crafting such an eye-catching cover for this book. And last but not least, thanks to you wonderful readers who chose this book! I wouldn't have my dream job if it wasn't for you, and I hope you have lots of fun with Officer Chastity "Cha-Cha" Rinaldi and Newton Isaac!

Chapter One
Rookie Blues

I leaned against the back wall of the small conference room, deferring to the senior officers who claimed the cushy rolling chairs. It was my first morning roll call as a rookie cop for the Mobile, Alabama Police Department. We candidates who'd successfully completed the police academy had graduated the preceding Saturday evening at a formal yet routine ceremony that had taken place a couple of times a year since time immemorial. My chest, which was already sizable at a 40F bra size, swelled even more when the police chief pinned my badge to my uniform and saluted me. I'd never felt so proud of myself. The 800 hours of training had been comprehensive and challenging, not to mention much higher than the 520 hours minimum required by state law, but I felt fully prepared for whatever situations I might face as a law enforcement officer. *How naïve I'd been.*

Captain Lockhart, a balding and broad-shouldered black man who led the precinct to which I'd been assigned, addressed the group. "We've got a new officer on our beat. She was sworn in Saturday." He raised a hand to gesture in my direction. "Everyone say hello to Officer Chastity Rinaldi."

A blush warmed my face as all eyes turned to me. I arced my hand in a demure wave, and gave them a greeting that expressed both my Italian and Alabamian heritage. "Buon giorno, y'all."

My fellow officers responded variously. A couple waved back. Several murmured words of welcome.

One hollered, "Fresh meat! Boo-yah!"

The officer next to him snickered. "I see an Italian, but it ain't got no sausage."

Sexist jerk. Lest my first name solidify with my new coworkers, I said, "I go by Cha-Cha."

The ruddy-faced guy who'd made the "sausage" comment hooted and hollered, "Whiskey, tango, fox trot, Cha-Cha!" He put one hand up and circled another in front of him, as if holding an invisible dance partner, and performed an improvised cha-cha in his chair. He hooted again, as if he thought his joke was not only hilarious, but original. It was neither. He clearly considered himself a comedian but, just as clearly, his coworkers did not. They responded with eye rolls and shaking heads. *There's one in every workplace.*

Captain Lockhart glared from under his brows. "Can it, Officer Stassney." Returning his attention to the group at large, he said, "Officer Rinaldi will serve in our motor unit."

The eyes of my fellow officers turned to me again, more curious this time. It was rare enough to have a woman join the ranks—only about 15% of law enforcement in the U.S. was female—but to have a woman officer who patrolled on a motorcycle was almost unheard of. I could deal with it, though. I'd been raised with three older brothers and had long ago learned how to make my way in what was predominantly a men's world. I considered myself more of a rare treasure than an oddity.

My academy training had taught me that, while all police officers had the same powers, the experiences of officers varied widely depending on whether they patrolled primarily on foot, bicycle, motorcycle, or in a cruiser. While an officer in a squad car could carry rifles, evidence collection supplies, and even stuffed animals to calm traumatized children at domestic violence calls, cops patrolling on foot, bikes, or motorcycles couldn't carry as much equipment and were limited to the bare essentials. We couldn't transport suspects, either, and would need to summon a patrol car to serve this purpose. The face-to-face interactions between the public and cops on foot or bikes gave those officers a bigger role in community relations, while motorcycle cops tended to handle a greater share of traffic matters. Even though traffic patrol wasn't the most respected part of police work, it was a critically important function. Besides snarls and delays, a reckless or distracted driver could cost someone their life or cause life-altering injuries. Enforcing the motor vehicle code was a valiant pursuit.

Captain Lockhart wrapped up the roll call with what I would soon learn was his standard send-off. "Protect and serve, stay safe, and be an honor to your badge. Officers dismissed."

I set out that morning feeling both nervous and excited to be patrolling on my own for the first time. No training officer. No one looking over my shoulder to observe. No one reviewing my paperwork to make sure it was correct and complete. Just me, my radio, the weapons on my tool belt, and my Honda ST1300PA police bike. Large 31 millimeter intake valves and 27 millimeter exhaust valves fed a combustion chamber with a 10.8:1 compression ratio. *As if I have any idea what that means.* I'd read it in the owner's manual, but it was gibberish to me. I knew squat about engines. But I did know the bike was sleek, powerful, and awfully fun to have between my thighs.

Having started with minibikes when I was only seven years old, I was an expert rider. My father and brothers had showed me how. Realizing she couldn't keep us off the fun bikes, my mother settled for making sure her children wore the best-rated helmets and every piece of safety equipment available. She also sent up prayers to every deity that might be in existence to keep our bones unbroken and our brains unscrambled.

I left the station that morning and set out on Interstate 10, which runs from Los Angeles, California all the way to Jacksonville, Florida, taking a curve around Mobile's coastline on its way through Alabama. It was a cool morning in mid-November. Despite the chill, I was sweating inside my uniform, partially because the poly-blend fabric didn't breathe well and partially because I was nervous as heck. The power I had as a police officer was enormous, but along with great power comes great responsibility. I wanted to wield it the right way, to do my job in a way that made people feel respected rather than bullied, to be fair and effective. Pretty heady stuff for a twenty-two-year-old who'd graduated mere months before with a criminal justice degree from the University of Alabama. *Roll tide!*

I headed east into the morning sun, riding only a mile or so and feeling horribly self-conscious before I spotted a dented, rusty horse trailer attached to a pickup truck up ahead, one lane to my right. The trailer was one of the fully enclosed styles. The small windows on the trailer had darkly tinted glass. All were closed. Either there were no horses inside, or the driver believed the morning to be cool enough to keep his equine cargo comfortable without ventilation. As the truck braked in the rush-hour traffic, only the right taillight on the trailer illuminated, glowing bright red. *The left one's busted.* Without properly functioning lights, the trailer posed a risk that someone coming up from behind wouldn't realize it was slowing down. They could rear-end it. *Better let the driver know there's a problem.*

I signaled to pull over behind the trailer and switched on my flashing lights. The driver of the pickup eyed me in his side mirror, his lids squinted to shield his retinas from the bright yellow orb just above the east horizon. His mouth moved, his lips clearly forming the F-word. But there was no need for profanity. So long as the guy didn't give me a hard time, I'd merely issue him a written warning and send him on his way. My stop would cost him a few minutes on the road, but it wouldn't cost him any money. I wasn't in the police game to fundraise for the city. I was in it to protect people and keep the peace. Even so, I came from a long line of hot-blooded Italian stock. If this guy gave me guff, I'd give him a ticket in return. It would only be fair.

The driver eased the truck and trailer over to the right shoulder and I followed him. I parked my bike behind him, slid off, and headed past the trailer to his window. The glass came down, revealing that the driver was not alone. Two other men sat shoulder-to-shoulder on the seat, the three of them packing the cab. All of the men were white. All were in need of a shave and a haircut. None of them was smiling. But hopefully I could change that when I released them without a citation.

The man at the wheel gave me a friendly, "How can I help you, officer?" But the cheery tone in his voice wasn't reflected in his eyes. Rather, like the busted taillight, they were dark and dull, devoid of brightness and light.

I lifted the faceplate on my helmet so I could speak with him. When he got a look at my face and realized it was a feminine one, his gaze shifted lower, to my chest. My oversized breasts were squashed smooth inside a sports bra and ballistic vest. Until I'd raised my faceplate, the driver had probably taken me for a barrel-chested man. It wasn't the first time, and it wouldn't be the last.

I gestured behind me. "You've got a busted taillight on your trailer, sir."

No sooner had the words left my mouth than sounds came from the trailer. Banging and clanging and high-pitched cries. While a horse might kick at the metal, no way could it cry out like that. I cast a glance back. The trailer rocked on its wheels. *What the—?*

Click-swish-creak. The driver seized on my distraction. In an instant, he unfastened his seatbelt, opened his door, and turned to slide out of the truck.

I raised my left palm in a *STOP* gesture, while simultaneously backing up and going for my belt with my right. "Stop, sir! Remain in your vehicle!"

But the man didn't obey. Instead, he reached back into the truck for the shiny silver handgun the man in the passenger seat held out to him.

HOLY SHIT!

Only minutes earlier, I'd been marveling at how my academy training had left me feeling confident and ready to face any situation. Now, it was everything I could do not to wet myself. Instinct took over, but so did the responses I'd practiced over and over, both during training and in front of a mirror at home. I whipped my pepper spray from my belt, aimed it into the cab of the truck, and jammed my thumb down on the spray button.

Cursing and coughing, the man in the passenger and middle seats shifted to their right. The driver, who was now outside the truck, had managed to avoid the brunt of the spray. He raised a fisted hand and swung at me, his curled hand landing just above my left ear. But while he had a mean right hook, I wore an even meaner helmet. The dumbass had reacted on instinct as well, rather than assessing the specifics of the situation. His fist was no match for my hard-sided helmet. *Kunk!*

Spewing curses, he cradled his shattered right hand in his left. Lest he pull a weapon or attempt another attack, I knew I had to disable him fast. Though I'd been trained well in takedown procedures in the police academy, I'll been trained even earlier by my older brothers and father. *A knee to the nuts renders any man powerless.* My knee went up and the man went down, hard, falling to his knees on the shoulder of the interstate. He buckled in two, simultaneously retching and roaring in fury.

Despite his bruised knuckles, knees, and nards, he attempted to stand back up. A stupid move given that he was still reeling in agony and totally off-kilter. As he rose, he veered into the traffic lane. *HOOOONK!* The top of his head was promptly clipped by the extended side mirror of an RV. *CLANG!* His forehead exploded in blood and he fell backward, his skull conking on the asphalt.

Normally I was enraged when motorists didn't slow or change lanes when they saw me with someone pulled over on the shoulder. But today, not so much. The man had somehow managed not to get knocked out cold. He was merely stunned, groaning as he lay on his back. I took advantage of his disorientation to grab his feet and drag him out of traffic. Before he could gather his wits, I knelt down, rolled him over, and cuffed his hands behind him.

The driver dealt with, I pushed the button to activate my helmet radio. "I need help!" I shrieked. "Backup and an ambulance! Suspects are armed!"

Once dispatch confirmed my location and assured me assistance was on the way, I glanced around for the two men who had fled the truck. Though things had occurred in rapid-fire motion and only thirty seconds had passed since the driver slid out of his truck, the other two men had made quite a bit of progress, despite being doused with the pepper spray. They'd nearly reached the top of the steep embankment flanking the interstate. *I have to stop them!*

I yanked my gun from my belt and hollered. "Stop and surrender!"

The one with the gun turned and aimed it in my general direction. Blinking to try to clear his eyes, he pulled the trigger and fired at random. The semi-automatic showered the pickup and trailer with bullets, the air filled with the *pop-pop-pop* of ammunition fired and the resulting *ping-ping-ping* of metal on metal. *Pop-ping! Pop-ping!* One bullet grazed my helmet. Another grazed my left arm, just above the elbow, cutting a swath through the fabric of my uniform and the first three layers of my skin underneath.

With his gun aimed down at the interstate and his eyesight blurred by pepper spray, there was a high probability a bullet would hit a passing motorist if he kept shooting. Whoever was in the trailer had already taken fire, and could be bleeding out right now. Though every instinct told me to take cover, I had to fight my natural reflexes. *I have to stop him! I have to shoot back!*

Most police officers never even draw their guns. But here I was, on my first stop ever, having not only to draw my gun, but use it. My gut clenched as I aimed my gun at his chest and pulled the trigger. *Low, as usual. Damn it!* I'd hit his inner thigh. Judging from the amount of blood spurting from the wound, the bullet had opened his femoral artery. His arms went up as he looked down and his gun continued to fire, spewing a barrage of bullets into the sky. *POP-POP-POP!* The man lost his balance and fell back onto the embankment. His buddy grabbed the gun from his hand and turned it on me. But while he had an advantage being up higher on the slope, I had gravity on my side. I shot at him and missed but, in his efforts to avoid taking a bullet, he tripped over his own feet, fell, and lost hold of the gun. Scramble and scrabble as he might, gravity got the best of him, dragging him down the steep incline, pulling him into an inescapable roll. He landed fazed and facedown at my feet, where I promptly straddled him, yanked his arms up behind him, and slapped my other pair of cuffs onto his wrists.

Sirens and squealing tires sounded behind me as my backup arrived. It was Officer Stassney. His mouth gaped when he saw my damaged helmet and the bullet holes in the trailer.

I directed him out of his cruiser and up the hill with a swing of my arm. "Get up there and cuff that guy!" I only had two pairs of cuffs and both were already in use.

While the man I'd grazed with the bullet made a desperate attempt to climb over the guardrail onto the frontage road, he was woozy from the loss of blood. Stassney tackled and collared him before he could climb over the railing.

The trailer continued to rock and the people inside continued to call for help, their cries even more desperate now. Some were in English. Some were in Spanish. With Italian and Spanish sharing common roots, I could understand some of the Spanish.

"Help us!"

"Let us out!"

"Please! Oh, God! Please, save us!"

"I'm coming!" I cried back. I searched the truck's console and found a key to unlock the padlock on the trailer door. Not easy to do with my hands trembling as if they held imaginary cocktail shakers. I finally managed to get the key into the hole and turn it. The lock dropped with a *clink* to the pavement. I swung the door open to find a dozen young women and girls crammed and cowering inside. The group included white, black, and brown females, ranging in age from around thirteen to thirty. They were terrified, exhausted, and bruised. There were at least four black eyes and two broken noses among them, courtesy, no doubt, of the dastardly, dumbass driver who'd swung his fist into my helmet.

I never saw anyone move so fast. The women and girls burst out of the trailer, crying and wailing. Some of them dropped to their knees as the pickup truck's driver had done, though they were on their knees to pray, not because they'd taken a knee to their nuts. Others grabbed me in tight bear hugs, overjoyed to be rescued from the clutches of those three creeps. One of the older ones spotted the driver handcuffed and sitting on the shoulder. She seized the opportunity to run over and slap his face with all the force she could muster. *Slap!* A bright pink handprint now adorned his cheek. *I hope it leaves a bruise like he left on them.*

Two of the women had been hit with bullets fired by the passenger from the embankment but, by either divine intervention or the firm hand of fate, the bullets had missed all of their vital organs and neither had life-threatening injuries. I called for another ambulance. Stassney loaded the uninjured man into his squad car, but stuck around until the EMTs had loaded the injured women, the driver, and the man I'd shot onto gurneys. Additional backup would escort the injured suspects to the hospital and keep them under guard. The women who didn't need medical attention were loaded into a paddy wagon for transport to the station, where they'd be questioned and their statements taken before they were released and reunited with family.

Before Stassney could drive off, I stepped in front of his squad car and held up a hand to stop him. He rolled his window down as I circled around to it. "See what I did here? No sausage needed."

He couldn't deny I'd handled the situation well. Hell, the mere fact that I was still standing said it all. "Well done, fresh meat." With that, he drove away, leaving me to ponder whether his pun had been clever or inadvertent.

#

An hour later, the women were being questioned by detectives in the conference room, and I was in Captain Lockhart's office reviewing for the umpteenth time what had happened that morning. My teeth chattered as the adrenaline processed out of my body, my uppers and lowers clapping painfully together. I blinked back the tears that threatened to spill down my cheeks. I was shaking so hard the gear on my belt jingled and gyrated like gold coins on a belly dancer's hip scarf. The confrontation, the shooting, the inured women. It was too much, especially for an unjaded rookie who'd simply expected to issue a few speeding tickets on her first day.

The captain finally sat back in his seat, satisfied that my story hadn't changed during the multiple retellings. He proceeded to bring up my dashboard camera and body cam footage on his computer screen. Thankfully, all I could see was the back of his monitor. I didn't think I could watch the images without totally falling apart. Still, I could hear my voice and the voices of the women. I sucked my lips into my mouth and clamped down tight to keep them from quivering.

My testimony and the video clip confirmed what I'd told him, that I'd followed proper protocols. If any shit hit the fan, he could point to long-established procedures so the flying fecal matter wouldn't land on me or him. His intense, pointed gaze softened as his facial features relaxed. "You did good, Officer Rinaldi. Kept the people on the road as safe as you could, and saved those women and girls from a rough life."

I didn't want to think of the horrors in store for them if the men had managed to get them to destination loaded into the truck's GPS. The walled-in compound in Florida was being raided by a SWAT team at this very moment. More rescues and arrests would undoubtedly ensue.

In what had to be the shortest shift on record, the captain said, "Take the rest of the day off, Officer Rinaldi. You've earned it."

#

Thanks to one of the young women having the forethought to surreptitiously break the connector to the left taillight as she and the others were forced into the trailer, I'd pulled the truck over. And, months later, thanks to the camera footage and the testimony of the women and girls, as well as that of yours truly, the three bastards were sentenced to life in prison. Billy Wayne Almstead, Trent Bosch, and Daytona Dickerson would never be eligible for parole, either. They'd been found guilty of a dozen counts of first-degree kidnapping, a class A felony, as well as another felony of assault in the first degree for their attempts to seriously injure or kill me. *Arrivederci, assholes!*

As the trial and sentencing ended and the men were being led in shackles from the courtroom, Daytona Dickerson, the driver of the pickup, turned back at the door, locked his evil eyes on me, and said in a creepily calm voice, "We'll get out, Officer Rinaldi. And when we do, we'll come for you."

I rolled my eyes. These guys were heading off to Limestone Correctional Facility, which sat near Huntsville in the northern part of the state. The facility was 360 miles away, about as far from Mobile as you could get and still be in the state of Alabama. They'd be under armed surveillance 24/7. No way would they escape. I met the man's threat with a healthy dose of snark. "Promises, promises."

Chapter Two
Love at First Citation

As expected, the three brutes had remained behind bars for over five years now. I, in turn, had remained on the police force during the ensuing half decade, issuing plenty of warnings for broken taillights, speeding, and other routine traffic violations, but never again uncovering a violent and extensive criminal enterprise. I had, however, been asked to repeat the story of my first rookie traffic stop for each incoming class of cadets. Without fail, the females chuckled and the men grimaced when I told them how I'd played hacky-sack with the pickup driver's scrotum.

When your very first traffic stop as a rookie cop ends with you uncovering an international human smuggling ring, facing a hailstorm of bullets from a semi-automatic, and ultimately arresting three violent brutes, every succeeding day can't help but feel a bit *meh*. Even so, I'd take *meh* over terrifying any day. *Who needs that kind of thrill?* If it turned out to be a once-in-a-lifetime event, that would be fine with me.

Today, I sat on my police motorcycle at a quarter before 8:00 AM and a quarter mile before a gas station on Highway 163. The spot was a great place to catch speeders. People running low on gas tended to accelerate in their efforts to reach a source of fuel sooner. It was an ironic and counterproductive response, as driving faster utilized more gasoline.

While I certainly hoped to keep the streets safe for motorists, I'll admit my motives were not entirely pure. The location provided a view of Mobile Bay and a fresh sea breeze. In early May, the mornings were still nice and cool. In another few weeks, they'd be hot and humid, and I'd be rethinking my decision to opt for a police bike rather than an air-conditioned cruiser. Made sense to enjoy these nice mornings while I could.

Speaking of speeders, here's one now.

An older red Prius hatchback zipped past me, my radar readout telling me the car was doing 67, just over the ten-mile-an-hour grace range that seemed to be an implicit social contract between the police and the public. Both hubcaps were missing on the passenger side of the Prius, and the rear fender had clearly taken a hit, an indentation spanning from the back bumper to the back door. I flipped on my lights and pulled out after the vehicle.

The driver slowed, signaled, and pulled to a stop on the shoulder. As I rolled up behind the car, the license plate caught my eye. FIZZIX. I pondered the plate's message. Did the driver work for a soft drink company? Was he a rap artist? Some sort of magician who performed at kid's birthday parties, sawing ladies in half and making things disappear? *One way to find out.*

I climbed off my bike, flipped up the faceplate on my helmet, and approached the driver's window. The glass descended, revealing the driver bit by little bit. Dark hair sticking up in casually haphazard spikes. Thick brows. Sexy brown eyes. A roguish grin formed by white, if slightly crooked teeth, and lips that looked utterly kissable. Broad shoulders covered in a blue button-down shirt that looked soft from repeated wear rather than stiff from starch spray. A bow tie printed with black and white penguins. The guy looked to be about thirty, just slightly older than I was now. He was much more attractive than the typical motorist but, while I might enjoy looking him over, I wasn't going to let his good looks influence me.

He cocked his head, his eyes narrowing slightly as he assessed my face. His grin widened. Either he was simply amused to realize a woman wore the helmet, or he liked what he saw. To my chagrin, I found myself hoping it was the latter. *Stay professional, Cha-Cha.*

When he spoke, his deep voice carried an authentic Alabama twang, the kind that made it sound as if his words were bouncing. "Dang. You caught me, Officer—" His eyes moved down to the nametag on my chest, but he didn't ogle me. "Rinaldi."

If he knows my name, I should learn his, too, right? "License and proof of insurance, please." I held out my hand.

"Sure." He leaned forward to pull his wallet from his back pocket. He slid his license out of the slot and handed it to me before reaching over to rummage through his glove compartment, which was crammed with papers.

I looked down at his license and fought a snort. "Your name is Isaac Newton?"

"Actually, it's Newton Isaac," he corrected me.

Duh. The familiar name had made me forget that driver's licenses are last-name first. "I guess I'm just used to seeing the name the other way."

"You're not the first to get it backward," he said. "My parents were both engineers at the Marshall Space Flight Center in Huntsville. They thought the name would be a tribute to their favorite scientist, but to most people it's a joke."

I could relate. A name could be a burden. When I was 13 years old and my chest seemed to develop overnight, boys in my class took to calling me "Chas-titties." *Buttholes.* Having the name Chastity also gave me a very difficult virtue to live up to, especially during the post-puberty years when my hormones were naturally raging. That's when I'd started calling myself "Cha-Cha" and insisting others do the same. But I wasn't about to share something so personal with a guy I'd just met.

I launched into my usual spiel. "Do you know why I pulled you over, Mr. Isaac?"

He cocked his head. "Was it A, because my registration is expired. B, because I was speeding. C, because my side mirror is missing, or D, all of the above?"

Is this guy giving me a pop quiz? "I'll ask the questions here."

"Sorry," he said. "Habit. I'm a teacher at East Mobile High School."

"Let me guess." I gestured to his FIZZIX license plate. "Physics?"

"Bingo!"

A gleam off something metal in his cargo bay caught my eye, and I looked back to see some odd contraption with wheels and gears and levers and tubes. "What's that in your cargo bay? Meth-making equipment? A moonshine still?"

He cast a glance behind him. "No. I'm no Walter White or moonshiner. I'm the faculty advisor for the school's robotics team. That's our robot, Geary. I took him home to charge his battery."

"Robot?" I fought a smile. "Maybe I should write you a ticket for excessive nerdiness."

"Ouch. That hurt." He put a hand to his chest as if in pain, but the sparkle in his eyes told me he was enjoying our little flirtation as much as I was.

I pointed to where the missing side mirror should be on his car, then the damaged fender. "Did the damage happen in the high school parking lot?"

"It did," he said. "Whose idea was it to give licenses to teenagers? Those kids can hardly handle a scientific calculator, let alone a vehicle. They should *not* be on the road."

"Tell me about it." I often made a point of positioning myself near the school in the mornings and afternoons just before classes started and just after they let out for the day. My presence encouraged the kids to slow down and drive carefully. *An ounce of prevention . . .* "You mentioned the mirror and your speeding. Did you also say your registration's out of date?"

"Expired at the end of the month."

I eyed his kissable mouth. "You know you have the right to remain silent, right? You don't have to incriminate yourself. Fifth Amendment and all that." *But if you wanted to whisper sexy words in my ear . . .*

"Dang." He shook his head. "Is it too late to retract my confession?"

"Yep." I walked to the back of his car to check his tags. Sure enough, they'd expired recently.

"If it helps," he called back to me, "I've got my check and registration paperwork right here." He held up an envelope. "I ran out of stamps. The team has been so busy after school getting the robot ready for competition that I haven't had a chance to get to the post office."

I stepped back to the window. "I can take that to the DMV for you, if you'd like." Their office was right across the street from the police station. I'd be returning there at the end of my shift and it wouldn't be any trouble to slip the envelope through their mail slot. Besides, my job was to protect and serve, right?

"You'd deliver it for me? Wow. Thanks! That would be great." He handed me the envelope before pulling out his wallet again. "I've got something for you in return."

I stiffened and stood up straight, wagging my finger. "Nuh-uh-uh. I don't accept bribes."

"It's not a bribe. On a teacher's salary, I couldn't afford to bribe you even if I wanted to." He reached into his wallet, pulled out a small blue ticket, and handed it to me.

I looked it over. It was a ticket for entry into a city-wide robotics tournament to be held in the high school's gym that weekend. I held it back out to return it to him. "Sorry. I can't accept anything of value."

"No worries," he said. "It's worthless."

"Worthless?"

Realizing what he'd said, he corrected himself. "I mean, the tickets are free. You don't even need one, really. Anyone who shows up will be allowed in. We're trying to draw a crowd. My robotics team works as hard as the football team. But does the robotics team get fans and cheerleaders? A pep rally? Does anyone decorate their lockers? No. Geeks get no love. It's a travesty."

I decided to show this particular geek some love by letting him off scot free. "To rectify that injustice, I'm going to let you go with just a warning, Mr. Isaac. The tardy bell rings soon and I don't want you to be late. But slow it down, all right? And get your mirror fixed."

"Thanks, Officer Rinaldi. See you at the robotics meet?"

"Sorry. Can't make it. I'm working Saturday." I handed the ticket back to him.

"Well, dang." He looked disappointed as he took it, but then he raised hopeful brows. "Maybe pull me over again sometime?"

"You better not give me a reason to. I won't go so easy on you again."

"Maybe I wouldn't want you to go easy on me."

When he wagged his brows, I fought a laugh. "Do you flirt with every police officer that pulls you over?"

"I do. The male cops act annoyed, but I secretly think they're flattered."

I swung my hand. "Get out of here before I change my mind and ticket you."

With a final smile, he rolled up his window, restarted his engine, and rolled along the shoulder until he could safely merge with the freeway traffic.

Chapter Three
Breakout

Thursday and Friday were typical days. Though I debated sitting near the school or patrolling the area where I'd seen Newton Isaac on the chance I might run into him, I decided against it. As much as I'd like to see the guy again, I didn't want to appear desperate or overly interested. Nothing turns a guy off faster than a woman that's too easy to catch. Besides, I had a date Friday evening with a promising guy I'd met on a dating app. He was a Fish and Game Warden for the Alabama Department of Conservation and Natural Resources. *Two law enforcement officers should have a lot in common, right?* And while he might not have been quite as attractive in his photo as Newton Isaac was in person, he was nonetheless a good-looking guy.

At 7:30 Friday night, I pulled my lime green Kia Soul into the parking lot of a seafood restaurant along Mobile Bay. I'd worn a high-necked blue dress with a loose, blousy top that helped to obscure the size of my bust. I'd learned the hard way that if I wanted to have intelligible conversation on a first date, my cleavage would have to be incognito, as it tended to turn men into blathering idiots.

I stepped into the restaurant and made my way to the bar, where I scanned the faces of those seated on the stools for the guy from the app. *There he is.*

He spotted me at the same time, raising a hand in greeting and sliding down from his stool, bringing his bottle of beer with him. "Cha-Cha?"

"Yep, that's me." I extended my hand for a shake. "Hi, Gunter."

We'd just introduced ourselves to each other when the hostess called his name. "Gunter? Party of two?"

She led us to a nice table on the patio. The ocean view, the sea breeze, and the setting sun created a perfect romantic atmosphere, and I felt hopeful that this night could lead to something. Unfortunately, the guy promptly spoiled any romantic mood by engaging in shop talk and regaling me with tale after tale of catching both commercial and recreational fisherman going over their limits, or fishing with only a regular license, not one specifically issued for saltwater fishing. *Could he be any more boring?* I attempted to steer the conversation in other directions by asking about his hobbies. *Fishing.* His childhood. *Son of a fisherman.* His dreams. *Win the Xtreme Bass Challenge fishing tournament.*

Gunter fished a hush puppy off his plate and waved it around as he detailed his most recent encounter with lawbreakers. "Nabbed two guys this afternoon, right out there." He jabbed the hush puppy in the general direction of Sand Island. "They brought in five red snapper against regulations. Red snapper season doesn't begin for three weeks."

I kept waiting for him to express some interest in me, my work, my thoughts and interests, to ask me something—anything!—about myself, but he paused his monologue only long enough to ask our server for more tartar sauce and to shovel more seafood into his mouth. After he'd discussed angling from all angles, it wasn't clear to me whether he was a self-important prig, obsessed with his work, or simply dull but, regardless, a half hour in I knew it would be our one and only date. I'd throw him back for some other woman to reel in.

My mind wandered, and I found myself wondering what Newton Isaac was doing tonight. *Is he having dinner with a fellow science teacher? Perhaps a biology teacher with whom he shares some chemistry?* I felt a twinge of jealousy I had no right to feel. After all, the guy had laid out the bait, but I hadn't taken the hook. *Sheesh. Gunter's got ME talking fish now.*

When the server returned, I asked for another glass of white wine. If I was going to have to listen to this guy drone on about gray triggerfish, spotted sea trout, and flounder, I'd have to numb my brain.

At the end of the night, I thanked Gunter for a pleasant evening. Luckily, he didn't inquire whether I'd be up for another date. He seemed to have as little interest in pursuing a relationship with me as I did with him. Perhaps I'd shown insufficient interest in the recreational and commercial creel limits. But, really, did any woman ever lean forward across the table and say *Tell me more?*

"Goodnight, Gunter."

"Take care, Cha-Cha."

After parting ways with him, I headed to my car and drove back to my house in the Driftwood Acres subdivision. My small brick home had been built in 1965 and encompassed less than 1,200 square feet, with three tiny bedrooms, one bath with chipped pink porcelain fixtures, and a narrow galley kitchen with its original green appliances. *They don't build them like that anymore.* It might not be the most beautiful residence in town, but what the outdated house had going for it was an affordable mortgage. Plus, while it didn't offer a view of the ocean, it was close enough to the coast that, if I breathed deep enough, I could detect a slight scent of salty sea spray. I'd take what I could get on my public servant's salary.

I parked in the carport and entered through the side door, which took me into the kitchen. I was met there by Brillo, my wiry gray Schnauzer mix whose coat resembled steel wool. At his flank was his sidekick, my white and ginger cat Knuckles, so named because the orange stripes across his white toes made it appear as if he wore brass knuckles. I'd adopted them from the local shelter after I'd bought the house. They'd been found roaming the streets of Mobile together, an odd but bonded pair, and the shelter had hoped to find them a home where they could stay together. I'd obliged, having gone into the place unsure whether to choose a dog or a cat to keep me company. By adopting both, I'd avoided the difficult decision.

"Hey, dudes," I said by way of greeting. I ditched my purse on one of the dinette chairs and reached down with both hands to ruffle their ears. "The date was a bust, in case you were wondering. All he could talk about was fish."

Knuckles cocked his head. *Fish* was a word he knew well. He probably hoped for a dollop of his tuna paté.

Knuckles trotted along beside me as I headed to the backdoor in the living room to let Brillo out for a tinkle in the postage-stamp-sized backyard. The dog did his business on the only tree, a scraggly pine. He sniffed around for a bit to determine what sort of vermin had dared to travel through his domain while he'd been stuck inside, unable to defend it from roaming marauders such as squirrels and raccoons. His potty break and patrol completed, he returned to the door and came inside.

I changed out of my dress and into my pajamas, washed my face, brushed my teeth, and flopped into bed. Given that I was scheduled to be on the job at 8:00 in the morning, I didn't stay up much longer, though I did watch the late news to see whether anything of concern was happening in the world. Just the usual wars, sports, and weather. The meteorologist forecast a sunny and mild day tomorrow, no chance of rain or high winds. *Exactly what a motorcycle cop wants to hear.*

#

Brillo woke me around 4:30 in the morning with a low growl, but the sounds from outside told me he was merely responding to the neighbor across the street arriving home from his bartending job. No need for worry. The three of us fell promptly back to sleep. We got up when the alarm went off at 7:00, stretched in synch, and hopped out of bed. After a quick shower, I slipped into my uniform, slicked my dark hair back into a low bun that would sit below my helmet, and slapped on a little makeup so I could look both pretty and professional. I fed both my pets and myself, and removed the safety panel from Brillo's small doggy door so that he could let himself in and out as needed throughout the day.

After giving both of my boys a kiss on the head, I headed off to morning roll call. It was routine. The sergeant on weekend duty reminded us all that a CPR refresher course would be offered next month, and that we should sign up if interested. He also asked us to increase patrols near a construction zone where thieves had made away with some building materials. Finally, he threatened for the umpteenth time to revoke refrigerator privileges for the person who had, once again, forgotten their leftovers in the station's refrigerator until they turned green and hairy and stunk up the place. Of course, the culprit had yet to be identified. Whoever it was didn't label their containers.

I pointed out the obvious. "We can solve this crime. Just fingerprint the containers already." Our prints were in the system. All of us officers had been fingerprinted when we'd been hired, so that the lab could readily identify and disregard our prints when analyzing evidence obtained from a crime scene.

The sergeant grunted. "The lab's busy. I'd rather not burden them with internal matters." He ran an accusing glare over the group. "But if this happens again, I'll do it."

Roll call concluded, I went outside and climbed onto my bike in the station's lot to begin my patrol. As I used my feet to ease my motorcycle backward out of the parking spot, my eyes shifted to the north, where scattered gray clouds scuttled by. *So much for the pleasant forecast.* I'd better keep an eye on the weather in case a storm decided to gather. High winds and wet roads could mean real danger for a motorcycle cop.

The shift was slow Saturday morning. The residents of Mobile seemed to be sleeping in. *Lucky ducks.* Few cars were out and about, and the drivers of those vehicles obeyed the speed limits and traffic signs and signals. Things being slow, I decided to cruise the streets along the waterfront, breathing in the salt air and watching the seagulls swoop and dive over a fishing boat as it returned from trawling the waters just off the coast.

Shortly after 10:00, dispatch came over the radio. "Officer Rinaldi, return to the station, please. Captain Lockhart would like to speak with you."

My sphincters reflexively clenched. *Uh-oh.* Why was I being called to the captain's office? Had I screwed up somehow? I mentally ran through the events of the last few days. Nothing struck me as out of the ordinary. No motorist was exceptionally belligerent when I issued them a ticket. They'd expressed only the standard amount of belligerence. Nobody had threatened to file a complaint against me or "take my badge." In fact, the only thing that stuck out to me at all was when I'd stopped Newton Isaac. *Who knew physics teachers could be so attractive?*

Maybe I was worried for no reason. Maybe the captain was calling me to his office to relay some good news. Maybe he'd decided to order that trunk-style saddlebag I'd been begging him for. I carried my department-issued laptop in my regular saddlebag, but I had to rest it on my seat to use it. It was an awkward position and risked the device slipping off. A trunk-style storage space mounted behind my seat would give me a flat, secure surface to serve as a mobile desktop. It would also give me a place to store more equipment, maybe some flares or traffic cones.

My department-issued cell phone vibrated and pinged with an incoming text. I glanced at the screen. It was a be-on-the-lookout alert, what we referred to as a BOLO. Rather than keep the captain waiting, I slid the phone back into my pocket. I'd take a look at the alert after our meeting.

Ten minutes later, my bike was parked in a spot near the front door of the station and my butt was parked in a seat facing the captain's desk.

Never one to beat around the bush, Captain Lockhart scrubbed a hand over the shiny dome of his head and said, "There's been a prison break. Billy Wayne Almstead, Trent Bosch, and Daytona Dickerson snuck out of the Limestone Correctional Facility late last night."

It took a few seconds for my brain to catch up with his words but, when it did, my sphincter tightened once more and my bones turned to icicles. My mouth opened, but no words came out, only a squeak. *Promises, promises.* The men had escaped from prison, as promised. The only question now was, would they keep their promise of coming for me?

My terror must have been written on my face, because the captain said, "It's doubtful they'll come for you, Officer Rinaldi. They were on their way from Arizona to Florida when you nabbed them five years ago. They don't have contacts here in Mobile. The most likely scenario is that they'll head to Miami. They've got friends and family there who could help them out. They'll probably be more interested in evading capture than in seeking revenge on you."

"Probably?" I repeated.

The captain exhaled a sharp breath. "It seems unlikely they'd head down here to Mobile, but these guys aren't exactly Mensa material. They could be stupid enough to come after you. Who knows?"

"How did they escape?" I'd heard crazy stories. A woman who ran a program for prisoners to train dogs had snuck a prisoner out in a dog crate. A mother drove a semi-truck through four fences to create an escape route for her imprisoned son. A group known as the Texas Seven killed a prison maintenance worker and injured several others in a scheme to steal their clothing, wallets, and identification to launch an escape. They remained on the lose for several weeks afterward before being apprehended at an RV campground and hotel in Colorado. After successfully impersonating a prison inspector whose business card he'd managed to obtain, the infamous Frank Abagnale, Jr. walked right out of the main doors of the facility where he'd been incarcerated. Inmates had even escaped from Alcatraz by digging through the air vents with sharpened utensils stolen from the prison cafeteria, leaving dummy heads made from paper, soap, and hair from the prison barbershop resting on their pillows.

"They faked food poisoning," the captain said. "When they were in the infirmary, they attacked the nurses and doctor on duty and tied them up with medical tape. They stuffed gauze in their mouths and put tape over their lips, too. They changed out of their prison uniforms and into scrubs, and used the doctor's keycard to exit. They'd taken one of the nurse's key fobs and used her car to get away."

I gulped. "How long ago was this?" Huntsville was 360 miles away, but that distance could be covered in six short hours. *Could Almstead, Bosch, and Dickerson already be here in Mobile, lying in wait to ambush me?*

"Around midnight," the captain said. "The convicts took the doctor's and nurses' debit cards, and hit an automatic teller machine right away. They got fifteen-hundred dollars in cash before driving the car to an all-night laundromat in Huntsville and ditching it there." He went on to tell me that, while at the laundromat, the escapees stole clothing from a dryer. The man the clothes belonged to had been standing out front, talking on his cell phone. He hadn't paid much attention when the fugitives passed him on their way into the facility, but as they hustled out he noticed they were wearing his T-shirts and jeans, and were carrying a laundry basket with the rest of his clothes in it. "He shouted at them but they ran off, so he called in a report. The responding officers found the prison scrubs left inside the laundromat and the nurse's vehicle abandoned out front, and put two and two together. The nurses and doctor had been found tied up at the prison a few minutes earlier, so the police were already looking for the nurse's car. They got K-9s out to the laundromat as quick as they could, but it was rainy and the dogs lost the trail."

I knew from chatting with K-9 officers that running water could confuse the dogs by carrying scents away from their source. Wind could have the same affect.

The captain continued. "The guys used the doctor's credit card to obtain three bikeshare bicycles. The bikes haven't been found yet. They're probably dumped in a ditch somewhere."

"The men could be anywhere, then." It was a fact, not a question.

"They could," the captain agreed. "But every law enforcement agency in Alabama, Georgia, and Florida are keeping an eye out for them. Tennessee and Mississippi, too. The news sources, airports, bus depots, and trains stations have been notified, too."

The BOLO alert. I pulled my phone from my pocket and tapped the screen to read the message that had been sent just before I'd come here. Sure enough, the post informed officers to keep their eyes peeled for three prison escapees, and provided the men's names and mug shots. *What a bunch of butt-ugly brutes.*

"Be extra vigilant," the captain said. "Consider patrolling in a cruiser. A squad car would offer you more protection."

"No, thanks." While a cruiser might offer a cage of steel and glass around me, the patrol cars were far less maneuverable, couldn't accelerate as quickly as my motorcycle, and couldn't squeeze into small spaces if I needed to execute an evasive action. I preferred to stick with my bike.

"Your call," he said. "If and when I hear anything new, I'll be in touch."

"Thanks, Captain."

He gave me a nod, though the anxious gleam in his eyes wasn't exactly reassuring.

Chapter Four
Schooled

As I ventured back out to my bike, I found my heart pounding and my eyes darting around the area, searching for hidden threats. *Could the creeps be hiding in the bushes, hoping to spot me leaving the station? Or in the foyer of the DMV, eyeing me through the window?*

A postal carrier walked up and slid mail through a slot on the building's front, just as I'd done with Newton Isaac's car registration renewal a couple of days before. The thought took me back to the teacher and his casually spiky hair, his smart and sexy eyes, his offbeat sense of humor. East Mobile High was on my beat. Maybe I'd swing by on my lunch hour, check out that robotics tournament he'd mentioned. *I could really use a distraction about now.*

My cell phone pinged and jiggled with an incoming text. I consulted the screen. It was a group text, sent by my father but with my mother and brothers copied on it. My father had worked as a street cop for three decades in my hometown of Montgomery before taking a position in the department's training and recruitment division. Now, he scouted for qualified candidates to fill positions on the force and taught classes at the academy. He continued to receive emergency communications from his department, and had evidently read the alert about the men's escape. His text was in all caps and read: *THOSE BASTARDS BETTER NOT COME NEAR YOU OR THERE WILL BE HELL TO PAY!*

I had no doubt my father would tear the men limb from limb if they threatened me again, assuming he could get his hands on them. Dad had taken time off from work to provide me with moral support on the days I'd testified at their trial. He'd sat in the gallery, boring holes in the back of their skulls with his pointed gaze. When Daytona Dickerson muttered "nice rack, bitch" as I'd walked past the defense table after testifying, my father had exploded in anger. If not for me grabbing his arm to restrain him and the bailiff raising his palm and giving my dad the don't-make-me-have-to-stop-you look, he would have gone after the guy right then and there and beat him to a pulp on the courtroom floor right in front of the judge and jury. Swift justice.

I bit my lip to keep it from quivering, and responded to my dad's text with the kissy-face emoji and words of assurance. *Captain says they're probably headed to Florida. I'm sure they'll be captured soon.* I only wish I felt as confident as my text implied.

#

A little after 1:00, I turned into the parking lot of the high school. Thirty or so cars were in the lot, along with several big yellow school buses. The marquee out front read ROBOTICS BATTLE SATURDAY 9-5. GO BOTS!

The front doors of the school were locked but, when I circled around to the side, I found the double doors to the gymnasium propped open. Two women, a redhead and a blonde, sat at a table just inside the door. They were probably mothers of the school's team members. They stopped chatting and looked up as I approached, greeting me with warm smiles.

"Welcome!" said the redhead. "Here to see the robot battle?"

"I am," I said, though the honest answer would have been that I was here to see Mr. Isaac. I was drawn to him, as if by some unseen magnetic force pulling on the underwire of my bra.

The blonde held out a flyer. "Here's a schedule. The East Mobile team won both of their battles this morning. They compete again in fifteen minutes."

I took the schedule from her. "Thanks." Looked like I'd arrived just in time. I had no idea how long these competitions took, but I had 57 minutes remaining in my lunch hour. I'd see what I could before I had to head back out on the beat.

I wandered farther into the gym, noting clusters of parents and kids sitting in the stands. Some wore gear in their school colors and emblazoned with their mascots. But Newton was right. There were no cheerleaders to be seen. Some of the parents held homemade signs supporting their teams, though.

A ring had been set up in the middle of the gym. It appeared to be approximately twenty feet square, with stanchions at each corner and a black nylon belt stretched between them. It was reminiscent of a boxing ring, but without the padded floor. Though it was empty now, I surmised it was where the robots duked it out.

A small group of teenagers in assorted races, sizes, and genders was huddled in a corner, all dressed in the turquoise and black colors of East Mobile High. They hunched over, heads together, their arms draped over each other's backs in a sign of camaraderie and team spirit. A slightly taller head rose above the others, a head with spiky brown hair. *Newton.* A sizzle rocketed through my circuits, every cell in my body activated.

Rather than interrupt their pre-battle pep talk, I took a seat on the third row of the bleachers nearby. A few seconds later the East Mobile High huddle broke with a battle cry of "Whoop-whoop!"

Newton stood up. He wore a T-shirt bearing a cartoon logo of a bull shark, the school's mascot, along with jeans and black and white checkerboard pattern skate shoes. But rather than looking like a teacher who dressed casual in a vain attempt to appear cool to his students, he seemed at home in his clothes, a perpetual kid at heart.

While Newton stepped up to the ring and shook hands with the opposing team's faculty advisor, the kids on the team headed to their robot, which was parked along the back wall of the gym. A skinny black girl with long braids hanging down her back carried a controller in her hands. She pushed some buttons with her thumb and manipulated the joystick. Their robot Geary came to life, rolling forward from the wall to the edge of the ring.

Geary was triangular, with a wheel at the bottom of each point that could rotate 360 degrees, allowing the robot to go in any direction.

The robot had arms on all three sides. The arms were long, with an elbow-like joint in the middle. The arms ended with pinchers, like the devices small-time offenders used to pick up trash along roadways to satisfy their community service. Like the wheels, the pinchers could rotate in a full circle, as evidenced by them spinning as it moved forward. A globe sat atop the device, the surface painted in reflective silver paint to match the body. Big googly eyes had been glued to the globe and, where his mouth should be, the students had attached two opposing silver saw blades to look like teeth. They'd topped the entire thing with a curly rainbow wig. Geary looked nothing like R2D2 or C3PO, the only robots I was familiar with, but for an inanimate object he had a lot of personality. The bout would prove whether or not he was as formidable as the opposition team's robot, which resembled a canister vacuum with five wheels, two accordion-like arms mounted on either side, and a tall antenna on top.

As Newton turned to address the team once again, he spotted me sitting in the bleachers behind them. His head snapped back in surprise and his mouth spread in a big smile. My body warmed at his welcome reception. He raised a hand to wave. I returned both the wave and the smile, wondering if he'd heated up on seeing me like I'd heated up on seeing him. Turning back to the kids, he said something, probably wishing them luck, and exchanged high fives with each of them. He and the other faculty advisor stepped behind a line marked with blue painter's tape.

A woman in a black and white striped referee shirt lifted one of the nylon belts and retracted it so the kids could drive their robots into the ring. Once the robots were both in place, she returned the belt to the stanchion. The girl operating Geary extended her hand to the Asian American boy controlling the robot for the opposing team. Once the two had shaken hands, the referee counted down. "Three, two, one. Go!" She blew a whistle, too. *Tweet!*

The scattering of spectators cheered as the robots rolled forward a few feet to an empty plastic bin. The bin was surrounded by items the robots were evidently supposed to pick up and place in the bin. A tennis ball. A wooden spoon. A two-foot stretch of rope. Geary's controller appeared to be in extremely capable hands. The girl operating him managed to pick up all three items and place them in the bin in the time it took the boy to pick up the spoon. He'd bumped the tennis ball with his robot, and it had rolled out of the ring.

As the audience applauded both team's efforts, Geary headed back to base, pumping his robot arms in victory just as the team members were doing. They fisted their hands and moved them in semi-circles from hip to hip, chanting "Go, Gear-y! Go, Gear-y!" But after they'd celebrated their victory, they shook hands with the other team, who were good sports and took the loss in stride.

I glanced down at the program. Per the schedule, the winner of this round would go up against the winner of the next round at 3:00. I'd be back on patrol then and would miss the East Mobile High's next battle. *Darn.* The bout had been surprisingly exciting, and I was impressed to see how creative the kids had been in designing their robots.

After congratulating his team, Newton strode over, propping one leg up on the bottom bleacher and resting his forearms on it to address me. "Playing hooky from work, Officer Rinaldi?"

"I'm on my lunch break."

"Well, I'm glad you were able to come by, after all. What do you think?"

"Geary's a quite capable robot. Can I borrow him to clean my house?"

"I could arrange that. He's a member of the United Robot Workers Local 36, though. He'd demand union pay rates."

"Sounds fair."

He gestured toward a service window at the front of the gym, where two middle-aged fathers were working a snack bar. "Can I buy you lunch? The volunteers at the concessions stand make a mean basket of nachos. The cheese goo is fresh, too. I saw them open a new gallon-sized can this morning. Gotta love the flavor of sodium hexametaphosphate."

"You had me at goo," I said with mock dreaminess. "Nearly lost me at the hexameta-whatever, though."

We strolled over to the concessions stand, where Newton purchased two baskets of nachos, two sodas, and a bag of Skittles for us to share for dessert. It was a well-balanced meal. All of the junk food groups were represented. Soft drinks. Candy. Processed cheese. Empty carbs.

He angled his head to indicate the doors. "Shall we dine al fresco?"

"A gourmet meal and fancy words?" I fanned myself with my hand. "Careful, now. I just might swoon."

He swept his arm, inviting me to proceed him. Once we were outside, he led me over to a half wall that separated the sidewalk from the parking area. We took seats atop the brick. He activated the lighter app on his phone, and set it down between us. "Candlelight makes a meal more romantic."

I snorted a laugh. Unladylike, but I couldn't help myself.

Newton popped the top on his soda. "If we're going to dine together, Officer Rinaldi, I suppose you should tell me your first name."

"It's Chastity," I said, "but I go by Cha-Cha."

"Ah. Can you dance the cha-cha, too?"

It was an old line, but I'd forgive him for it. "Little bit." I slid off the wall and demonstrated the few steps I knew, moving forward and back as I counted the steps. "One, two, cha-cha-cha. Three, four, cha-cha-cha."

"Eh." He held out a flat hand and angled it left and right in a so-so motion.

I put my hands on my hips. "You think you can do better?"

"I *know* I can."

He slid down from the wall and showed me his moves. Dammit, he was better than me. By far, too.

"Where'd you learn the cha-cha?" I asked.

"Auburn," he said. "Rumor had it that the campus ballroom dance club was a great place to meet girls because they were always short on male partners."

"How'd that work out for you?"

He repeated his earlier routine, giving me an "eh" and the so-so hand motion. "Met lots of girls, but most of them stepped on my toes. I decided to try the dating apps after that."

"And?"

"It was only slightly less painful."

I could relate. I'd tried the dating apps, too. Most of the guys I'd met were either only looking for a hookup or they were odd ducks. A couple had been okay guys, just not right for me. Gunter, for example. I'd never made a cyber love connection. I wondered whether I'd make a connection here today, in the wild.

Newton and I chatted as we crunched our way through our nachos, stopping occasionally to lick melted cheese from our fingers.

"I'm curious." Newton slid me a sideways glance. "Why did you decide to become a cop?"

The choice of career said a lot about a person. Their personality. Their values. Their strengths and weaknesses. I shrugged. "I suppose it was a combination of factors. I grew up in a rough neighborhood in Montgomery with three older brothers. They taught me how to stand up to the bullies." Ironically, my brothers sometimes *were* my bullies, snatching the television remote out of my hand, shoving me aside as we raced to the kitchen when our mother called *Who wants the last brownie?* The usual big-brother stuff. "I saw some of the kids at school get picked on. They either didn't know how to defend themselves, or they were too scared to. It bothered me that the mean kids got away with tormenting the other kids."

"Did you do something about it?"

"Every time. I'd go stand between the kid being bullied and the bully and say 'bring it.'"

"And?"

"Nobody brought it. Called me an insulting name or two but just walked away. I guess they figured if I wasn't scared of them, maybe I had a good reason not to be." I shrugged. "Roughhousing with my brothers at home made me less fearful of a physical confrontation."

His head bobbed as he mulled over my words. "You said there were a variety of factors. What were your other reasons for becoming a cop?"

"I love motorcycles. Police work is the only job that pays you to cruise around on a bike all day. Plus, public service runs in my family. My father was a police officer in Montgomery, and my mother was a social worker. All three of my older brothers are in law enforcement. Two are cops, one is a deputy sheriff."

"Ah," Newton said, with a teasing twinkle in his eye. "You're a traditional girl."

Some of the kids from Newton's robotics team wandered out of the gym doors, interrupting our conversation. They stepped over, looking from Newton to me and back again.

A chubby white kid with a space between his front teeth asked, "Are you in trouble, Mr. I?"

Newton cut me a look. "Big trouble, I fear."

I greeted the kids. "Great job in there. Y'all built a very capable robot."

The girl who'd operated the bot said, "We couldn't have done it without Mr. I. He taught us how to design a robot and how to program it, too."

"You got that right, Tamika," Newton said in a shameless but teasing tone. "Sometimes y'all even listened to me."

The chubby boy grunted. "Not that time Chao overloaded the circuits."

The boy who must be Chao frowned. "At least the wheels I screwed on didn't fall off."

Newton emitted a sound like a penalty buzzer. *Errrt.* "No squabbling. We're a team, remember? Everybody screws up sometimes. Mistakes are how we learn."

Tamika groaned and rolled her eyes. "If mistakes are how we learn, then we should be the smartest team ever." Turning the conversation to their competitors, she said, "Did you see that robot with the caterpillar wheels? I've never seen a bot move that fast."

Chao said, "I'm more worried about the one with the legs. It's slow, but the arms are more maneuverable than ours."

I glanced down at my phone. As much as I would have liked to stay and see how their remaining bouts turned out, my lunch hour was nearly up and it was time for me to get back out on patrol. "I've gotta head out. Good luck in your other battles."

Newton and I gathered our trash and recycling, and carried the refuse to the bins near the gym doors. The kids followed us.

After discarding our items, Newton and I turned to each other to say goodbye.

He cut his gaze to the kids around him. "Buzz off, you brats. Can't you see I'm trying to get this pretty cop's phone number?"

"Ooh, Mr. I!" Tamika cried. "You gonna ask this lady on a date?"

"I plan to. Think she'll say 'yes?'"

The chubby boy looked from him to me and back again. "No, but I admire your confidence, Mr. I."

"Go." Newton made a shooing motion with his hands. "I'll catch up with you before the next round."

The kids walked off, giggling and casting knowing looks over their shoulders.

Newton turned to me. "I don't know why I put up with them." Despite his language, it was clear he enjoyed working with the kids and, despite the casual way they spoke to him, it was clear they respected and appreciated him. "So? Can I get your number, Cha-Cha?"

Chapter Five
Outgunned

I pulled my phone from my pocket. "What's your number? I'll text you my contact info."

As Newton rattled off his phone number, I typed it in and sent him my contact info in return. I was about to slide my phone back into my pocket when the ringtone began to blare. A glance at my screen indicated it was Captain Lockhart calling. *Maybe he has good news for me about the escaped convicts.* I glanced up at Newton. "I've gotta take this. It's my captain. See ya."

He gave me a nod and I turned, stepping a few feet away and stopping to take the call. I put a finger to my left ear to block out the noise of the robots battling in the gym and the kids and parents cheering them on. "Please tell me they've been captured," I said without preamble.

"Wish I could, Cha-Cha," the captain said in a rare use of my first name, a sign he realized how much this situation was weighing on me personally, not only as a police officer. "Unfortunately, I'm calling to let you know we received a report that three men fitting the description of Almstead, Bosch, and Dickerson robbed a gun and knife shop in Birmingham."

Birmingham. In other words, they'd were a hundred miles closer to Mobile now, still together, and armed. *But with what, exactly?* "What kind of weapons did they get?"

"A dozen semi-automatic rifles. As many or more handguns. Couple of shotguns. An arsenal of ammo." In other words, any law enforcement officers who ended up facing these lawbreakers would be horribly outgunned. But the captain wasn't done yet. "Silencers, too. They also took a bunch of hunting knives and punch daggers."

"Punch daggers. Hell." The close-contact weapon was a particularly nasty and vicious choice of weapon. The knife comprised a wide, sharp blade attached to a T-shaped handle that an attacker could clench in their fist and easily drive into the chest or gut of their victim, twisting it for maximum effect. If the fugitives came after me, I could only hope they'd use a gun, not a knife, to kill me, and that they'd make my death quick. The nachos squirmed in my stomach. "Did they hurt anyone at the store?" *Or worse?*

"They pistol-whipped the clerk something fierce. They hit as he was opening the store for the day and knocked him out cold before he could get to the alarm. They locked the front door and escaped out the back, but another customer who bought ammo at the store on a regular basis came by not long afterward. He tried the door, but it was locked. He thought it was strange that the store wasn't open yet when it was supposed to be. He looked through the glass and saw the clerk's foot sticking out from behind the counter, got help out there right away. Good thing, too. The clerk has a major brain bleed. Lord knows whether he'd have survived without prompt medical care."

In other words, the escaped fugitives had left the clerk for dead, not caring whether he survived. *Heartless, soulless cretins.* "Were they in a vehicle?"

"That remains unknown. Nobody saw them get into a car, but they had to get away somehow. Birmingham PD has a chopper in the air and the highway patrol has established roadblocks and checkpoints on every major road out of Birmingham."

While I knew our fellow law enforcement agencies would do everything in their power to catch the escapees, these men were proving to be uncommonly crafty. They couldn't have concocted and carried out an effective escape plan otherwise. Even if the highway patrol officers looked into every vehicle moving down the highway, the men might find a way to slip past law enforcement. The smart course of action would be to find a place in the city to hole up for a few days until the heat was off.

The captain said, "We've had requests from the media for an interview with you. We've turned them down. I don't think it's a good idea for you to show your face on television right now."

"I agree." Seeing me on TV might only further inflame the men, incite them to make good on their vow of vengeance. Besides, the department had a public relations office trained to handle media interactions and issue press releases. I'd leave the department's messaging up to the PR professionals.

The captain offered to put me up in a safehouse. "We could get you a hotel room, assign officers to stand guard."

Although I appreciated the offer, I knew most hotels didn't allow pets, and I didn't want to be separated from Brillo and Knuckles. The department's budget was already strapped, too. I didn't want to impose an additional, unexpected financial burden. Besides, even though the men had headed south, toward Mobile, chances were they'd intended to turn east on Interstate 20 in Birmingham and take that road to Atlanta, where they'd hop onto I-75 south to Florida. They probably wouldn't continue this way. That said, I didn't want to be stupid, either, and put myself or my pets at unnecessary risk. I suggested a compromise. "How about if we increase patrols by my house? Maybe park a spare cruiser out front?" Even if the fugitives intended to come after me, these tactics should either keep them at bay or result in their arrest.

The captain concurred. "All right. I'll get a spare squad car over to your place and instruct officers to swing by on a regular basis."

Fortunately, I worked in the same precinct that I lived, so the captain wouldn't have to coordinate with another division. My fellow officers knew me personally and we were all on good terms. Even the somewhat sexist Stassney and I had come to an understanding of sorts. They'd make sure to keep a close eye on my place. We ended the call and I slid my phone into the pouch at my waist. Lost in thought, I jumped when a voice came over my shoulder.

"What's going on?"

I turned to find Newton had walked up behind me.

He frowned in concern and raised his palms in confession and contrition. "Sorry. I wasn't meaning to eavesdrop, but I couldn't help but overhear your conversation. Something about weapons? And patrols by your home? And you wondering if—" He made air quotes with his fingers as he said, "'They've been captured?'" His eyes narrowed. "You're talking about those escaped convicts from Huntsville, aren't you?"

I sucked my bottom lip into my mouth, wondering how much to tell him. But then I realized my photo or video footage of me at the men's trial would soon be all over the news, if it wasn't already. "Yeah. You heard about that?"

"Saw a headline on my news app that they'd escaped." His eyes narrowed even further before suddenly widening, as if he'd had an epiphany. "Wait. You're *her*, aren't you?"

"Her who?" I asked, though I was fairly certain I knew what he meant. I was the *her* whose traffic stop five years earlier had led to the rescue of dozens of victims of human trafficking and the arrest of nearly as many creeps who'd been operating a sick, sadistic international crime ring.

"The rookie who got into a gunfight with three armed men on the freeway and sent them to jail."

I heaved a breath and nodded. "Yeah. That was me."

Dumbstruck, his mouth gaped. "Wow," he said, finally. "I didn't realize I was dealing with a celebrity."

I scoffed. "I'm not a celebrity. I was only doing my job."

"Maybe," he acquiesced, "but you did it darn well." As if realizing that the situation was fraught with emotion for me, he broke the ice with some humor. "Is it weird that I'm really turned on right now?"

I snorted another laugh. "I suppose that beats feeling emasculated."

"Hell, yeah," he said. "You inspired one of my female students to study criminal justice in college. You were her hero."

"Really?" My insides, which had only recently been squirming, warmed with the thought that I'd helped another young woman discover her calling. Frankly, I thought law enforcement could use more female officers. When a woman showed up, violent situations would sometimes deescalate, men reacting on instinct as they'd once reacted to their mothers, I suppose. At least the arrival of a female officer didn't add more testosterone to the mix, another dick to bang. People in trouble, especially kids and teens, seemed to open up more to female officers, to cooperate rather than resist.

Newton said, "You've got to let me take you to dinner tonight. Someplace fancy and expensive, worthy of a cop of your caliber. Maybe even somewhere with valet parking."

I pointed at his checkerboard shoes. "You'd have to change your footwear."

He looked down as if to remind himself what shoes he was wearing before looking up again. "I can dig out my loafers. Maybe even a pair of khakis and a sport coat." He cocked his head. "Does your questioning my shoes mean you've agreed to go out with me?"

I shrugged. "I suppose it does."

"Careful," he said, with a wry grin. "You wouldn't want your enthusiasm to give me a big ego."

I fought a grin of my own. I'd been thinking of the guy since I'd stopped him on the road earlier in the week. My showing up here today told him as much. I'd already tipped my hand, showed him I was interested. No sense appearing too overeager.

I gave him my address and he entered it into his phone app. "Seven o'clock good for you?"

"Sure."

"All right. See you then." He hiked a thumb over his shoulder and backed away. "I better get back in and check on my team."

"Good luck!"

I spent the rest of the day cruising my beat, eyeing the occupants of each car I passed to see if it might be the fugitives, and looking forward to my date with Newton. To my dismay, no additional information came in about the escapees. Wherever they were, they'd managed to elude law enforcement. I feared they were holed up somewhere, preparing their weapons and forming a plan. I was left to wonder whether those plans included me.

When my shift was over, I returned home, greeted my furry housemates, and fed them their dinner. After I'd showered and applied fresh makeup, I stood before my closet, trying to decide on an outfit. Newton had yet to ogle my breasts, a big point in his favor. Maybe I'd wear something a little more form-fitting than I usually chose for a first date. *Hmm . . .*

I eventually decided on a lavender A-line dress and a pair of wedge sandals. I pulled the bobby pins out of my bun and let my hair fall free, shaking it loose and adding a little curl with a curling iron.

Newton arrived promptly at 7:00. He'd cleaned up nicely. He was dressed in the khakis and a tan sport coat, along with shiny loafers and a crisp white dress shirt. He smelled good, too, like some type of citrusy body wash. He held a small bouquet of flowers in his hand, pink roses with something purple and stalky mixed in. He eyed my loose hair, my dress, and my shoes, a smile playing about his lips. "You look very different out of uniform."

I smiled at his clumsy compliment and reached out to take the flowers from him. "How sweet. Come on in. I'll put these in some water."

He looked down at Brillo and Knuckles, who flanked me on either side, standing stiffly and staring up at Newton as if in challenge. "Is it safe for me to step inside?"

"Back off, boys," I ordered my pets in my authoritative cop voice. "Newton's a good guy."

As if to prove my point, Newton knelt down and let both of my pets give his shoes and knees a thorough sniff. "Am I approved?" Newton asked them after a few seconds. Brillo wagged his tail in response, while Knuckles merely sauntered off, no longer concerned that Newton posed any sort of threat. Newton scratched Brillo under the chin, and the dog raised his snout and closed his eyes in bliss before his back leg lifted in a reflexive response and did an air scratch.

Newton stood and gestured behind him. "I saw the empty squad car out front. Is it a decoy?"

"It is," I admitted, "but the captain's got patrols running by here every half hour, at least. If the men I sent away are going to come after me, we're not going to make it easy on them."

I retrieved a glass vase from a cabinet in the kitchen, added some water, and arranged the flowers. I carried the vase to the living room and placed it on my coffee table. The flowers' lovely scent and splash of color brightened the space.

I turned my attention back to Newton. "How'd the rest of the battles go? Did Geary win?"

"Nope. We lost. But it was close. We'll beat 'em next time."

"That's the spirit."

A half hour later, we were seated at a corner table in an authentic Italian bistro downtown, a bottle of red wine on the table and real candlelight flickering between us rather than imitation candlelight from Newton's phone. After ordering, we sipped our wine and chatted amiably. I asked Newton about his path to becoming a high school teacher.

"I didn't initially set out to become an educator," he admitted. "After I got my degree in physics, I went to work for Raytheon. It wasn't a bad job. It paid well. But it was very . . ." He looked up as if searching for the right term. "Sterile, I guess you'd say. My coworkers were serious about their work, as they should be, but none had a sense of humor and most were introverts. The atmosphere felt stifling to me. I was around physicists all day, and it felt insular. I didn't want my life to be so narrow. I got in touch with my high school physics teacher to see if he had any advice. He always seemed to love his work, so I thought he'd be able to give me some guidance. He asked if I'd ever considered teaching. He thought my demeanor would be well-suited for it. I wasn't sure, at first, so I signed up to substitute to see if I'd like it. I was surprised by how fun it was, how much I enjoyed making science interesting for kids. I went back for my teaching certificate and here I am, six years and sixty grand less in annual salary later."

I had to laugh at that. "Work isn't all about the money." If it were, I wouldn't have gone into law enforcement. I could have earned much more doing something else, too.

He tore off a bite of garlic bread. "I supplement my salary by leading rocket-building workshops at the rec center summer camp. The kids love it. More and more girls sign up each year. The push to get more women into STEM careers seems to be working."

"Glad to hear it." I was all for women pursuing their personal interests without pressure to conform to an outdated notion of a woman's place in the world.

He told me about some of the more creative science fair projects his students had come up with, and asked about unusual crimes I'd come across.

"I once arrested a beautician who was performing illegal Botox injections at her salon. Her clients were happy until one of them ended up with a bump between her eyes that was shaped like a crunchy Cheeto." I went onto tell him about a man who went door to door on Halloween dressed as a vampire, only to whip open his cape when unsuspecting residents opened their doors and "treat" them to a peek at his privates. "The booking officer forgot to have the guy remove his fangs before taking his mug shot. The photo is still hanging in the station."

I also told him about the time a silent motion-detector alarm had been triggered at a jewelry store, and that I and two other officers arrived to find the thieves still at work, their bodies wrapped in aluminum foil. One of them was an employee. He'd known there were motion-sensing alarms in the place, but he'd thought the foil would reflect the beams and negate the signal.

Newton groaned. "Idiots."

"Some criminals are," I agreed. "But some are quite clever." I'd always wondered why the smart ones used their intellect for evil when they could apply it to something good. While poverty and mistreatment could lead to crimes of desperation and illegal drug use, some criminals had no good reason for committing their crimes, other than to see if they could get away with it. Why risk incarceration? Were they looking for a thrill? Were they sociopaths, or simply born pre-wired to defy social norms?

After our food arrived and we dug in, Newton cut me an intent glance. "I'm curious. What made you change your mind and come by the high school today?"

There didn't seem to be anything to lose by being honest. "I had a really lousy date last night."

"Oh, yeah? Lousy how?"

"All the guy could talk about was his work. He's a game warden for the state. It was fish, fish, fish all night long. He never once asked me anything about myself." I sighed and picked up my wine glass. "What about you? Met anyone interesting lately?"

"Only you," he said. "I've made my way through the apps. I had an okay time with a few of the women, but nothing special. Some lost interest once they saw my crappy car and realized I'd never be the sugar daddy they're looking for. Saved me the trouble of ghosting them for being gold diggers."

"It's a brutal dating world," I concurred.

"I decided to forget the apps and leave it to fate." He angled his head and gave me a small smile.
"Gotta say, fate is working out much better."

My face warmed from the flattery.

We finished our meal and took a drive out to Mobile Bay, where we sat on the sand and talked into the wee hours of the night. Unlike Gunter, Newton didn't bore me, not even once. When we finally returned to my house, it was after 2:00 AM. We stopped on the porch. Brillo barked inside until I shushed him. He proceeded to sniff around the inside of the front door. *Snuffle, snuffle, snuffle.*

I turned to face Newton. "Thanks for dinner."

"It was my pleasure," he said. "So is this." He moved forward and lowered his head, treating me to a warm, soft kiss that gave every atom in my body a positive charge. When he finally backed away, he said, "Let's do this again. Soon."

"I'm game."

Eyes gleaming, he gave me a grin and turned to go.

I went inside and closed the door behind me. Brillo and Knuckles looked up at me as if to ask *Well? How was it?* I responded by doing a happy dance.

Before going to bed, I checked with the station to see if there were any updates on the escaped convicts that I might have missed. "Any news?" I asked the officer on desk duty that night.

Unfortunately, there was nothing new. The men hadn't been spotted since they'd fled the gun and knife store. "Wish I could tell you different."

"Me, too. But we'll get them. Sooner or later." It was the *later* option that concerned me. How long might it take to catch the creeps? And was I fooling myself to think recapturing them was inevitable? After all, some suspects in long-ago crimes remained on the loose. It had taken sixteen years for the FBI to find killer Whitey Bulger, and they'd only caught up to him thanks to a tip from a discerning neighbor. Television shows like *America's Most Wanted* had been a big help in catching many who'd fled from justice, but some criminals had remained on the FBI's most-wanted list for decades.

I told myself for the hundredth time that the captain was probably right. The fugitives were most likely headed to Florida. Even so, they might decide to swing by Mobile for a reunion with me first. It would be easy for the men to find me. After all, they knew where I worked. Property information was public record and accessible online, so they could easily determine where I lived, too. While Brillo was a world-class watchdog and would warn me if anyone came into the yard, he was much too small to serve as a guard dog. Even if he could attack, I'd never put his life at risk like that. It was my duty to defend us and our home. To that end, I placed my service revolver in quick reach on the nightstand, just in case the men decided to come by tonight and make good on their promise.

Chapter Six
Home Security

The Birmingham roadblock was called off twenty-four hours after it was instituted, proving to be too great a hindrance to the flow of traffic and ineffective for catching the men, who had either holed up in the city or somehow sneaked out of the area, possibly on a small country road or on foot across fields.

The captain called to give me the news. "This doesn't mean the highway patrol is giving up," he assured me. "They're going to fly choppers along the main arteries to look for anyone who appears to be traveling on foot. The fugitives' faces are going up on digital billboards throughout Alabama and the southeast, too."

It was little comfort. Though I told myself the men would have to be crazy to come for me, fear kept bubbling up in me, eating away at me like emotional acid.

My parents called me via Facetime late Sunday afternoon, their features tight.

My mom looked like she hadn't slept a wink. "Take leave and come home," she said. "You'll be safe here."

"I'll also be broke." I had a mortgage, a car note, and student loans to pay. I could barely cover them as it was. If I missed out on a week or more of pay, my finances would be in trouble.

My father leaned into the phone, forcing my mother's face aside. "You know we'll help you out if you need it, Cha-Cha."

"I know, Dad," I said. "But you've got your retirement to think about. You don't need me back on your payroll."

Frowning, my father turned to my mother. "She's just as stubborn as ever."

My mom then turned on my father. "She gets that from you."

"No, she doesn't."

I chimed in. "Yes, I do, Dad."

He turned back to the screen. "Well, that's a fine how-do-you-do!"

Mom and I exchanged a knowing glance over the airwaves. I comforted them as best I could. "I'll be okay. Brillo will let me know if anyone approaches the house. You know what good ears he has." When that seemed to appease them a little, I took things further. "I'll install some motion sensor lights outside and a security system with video cameras." Maybe I'd get a system with interior cameras, too, the kind with speakers I could talk through remotely. If the fugitives somehow broke into my house while I was away, I could at least curse them out if I couldn't fill them with lead.

My parents sufficiently satisfied to drop the subject, we caught up on the latest family gossip and news from the old neighborhood before ending our call.

I set my phone aside and rounded up my computer to research home security systems. The complexity and cost varied widely, from a single-camera wireless doorbell model that cost less than $100, to multi-camera systems with backup batteries and motion-detection sensors that cost several grand, not including installation. Putting a system in my house could use of every bit of my meager savings. What's more, it could take several days to get someone out to wire the system.

Newton was the only person I could think of who would know how to install a security system and be available to do it quickly. After all, he'd taught the kids how to build, wire, and program their robot. Maybe I could pay him to put a system in. He'd mentioned that he taught kids how to build rockets at a summer camp for extra money. Sounded like he could use the income. I sent him a text. *I'm going to put in a security system at my house. Got any recommendations and can I impose on you to install it? I'll pay you for your time.*

Rather than text me back, he called. "I feel incredibly sexy right now. It's not often a nerd gets a chance to be a hero, especially to a cop."

"You better jump on it."

"Hell, yeah! How 'bout I swing by in a few minutes and we'll hit the electronics store? We've got a couple of hours before they close."

"I'll be waiting."

Newton picked me up and we drove to the nearest electronics store. He looked over several systems, carefully reading their technical specifications and translating them into non-geek for me. "This one has stationary cameras with a one-hundred-and-eighty-degree field for the lens. That'll work well up against the house. For the inside, I'd suggest the ceiling mount style. They've got a full range of vision and can take in the entire room. I'd suggest you get a hidden backup in case they disable the main camera. The smaller nanny-cam types can be hidden on a bookshelf or mantle."

When we left the store, I'd spent nearly $500 on cameras, but I hadn't just bought equipment, I'd bought some peace of mind, too. Still, while a camera and alarms could provide me with a warning that the escaped cons were approaching my place, the devices wouldn't stop them from getting in and doing away with me. After all, it took ten minutes on average for law enforcement to respond to an emergency call. A lot could happen in ten minutes. Bank robbers could empty a half dozen teller tills and drive off in their getaway car. A house could be stripped of its silver, fine jewelry, televisions, and laptops. A buxom female cop could absorb a hundred rounds of ammo at point-blank range or have a punch dagger stabbed into her heart. The mere thought had my blood-pumping organ crawling into my throat.

Back at my place, I ordered Chinese takeout for dinner, while Newton set about installing the system under the watchful eyes of

Brillo and Knuckles. Newton took a break to eat with me, dipping his egg roll in both the hot mustard and the orange sauce, the same as I did with mine. Looked like the two of us had even more in common than I realized.

When he returned to work, I helped as much as I could. I passed screws and tools up to him as he stood on one of my kitchen chairs to install the camera on the ceiling. I gathered up the packaging to toss out or recycle. I recited my wifi password so he could connect the devices to my internet service.

When the installation was complete, he said, "I need to test the alarm. It might scare Brillo and Knuckles."

"I'll take them out to my car." The sound would be muffled inside my vehicle, and they wouldn't be able to run off, either.

I retrieved the cat carrier from the coat closet. *Rrrowrr!* Knuckles growled and went spread eagle when I tried to put him into it, but eventually I wrangled the rascal inside. Brillo happily allow me to attach his leash, thinking we were going for a walk. Instead, I took them out to my car, loaded them inside, and backed out of my driveway, heading halfway down the block to wait while Newton tried the alarm. The *woo-woo-woo* was audible outside for about three seconds before he switched it off. I hoped it hadn't annoyed the neighbors. I drove back to my house, parked in my carport, and took my pets back inside.

With the alarm confirmed to be in working order, he tested things out on both my computer and my phone, making sure I could log in to the live feeds and that the voice connection worked properly.

He handed my phone to me and circled his finger. "Say something. Let's make sure we can hear it."

"Testing," I said, my voice coming through loud and clear on the speakers. "One, two, three." Still broadcasting through the speakers, I cut my eyes to Newton and said, "Thank you so much. You don't know how much I appreciate this."

He cocked his head and sent me a sexy grin. "You could *show* me how much."

I lowered my phone from my mouth. "Not after one date, buddy."

"I see," he said. "You're gonna make me work for it."

Hell, yeah. "Speaking of working for it." I went over to my purse on the coffee table and pulled out my checkbook and a pen. "How does two-hundred for the install sound?"

He waved a hand. "Uh-uh. No way am I taking any money from you."

"But you've been here all evening."

"I enjoyed every second of it."

Aww. A warm sensation flooded me. This guy sure knew how to lay on the charm.

I helped him gather his tools and return them to his toolbox. Brillo and I walked him out to his car to say goodnight.

After he'd loaded his toolbox into his cargo bay and closed it, he turned to me, put a hand on either side of my waist and pulled me closer, almost touching but not quite. I had no idea what you'd call the force spanning the small distance between us, but it was charged and nearly palpable. Maybe one day the two of us would create some friction.

He leaned down and gave me another kiss, this one longer, warmer, and deeper than the one he'd given me the night before. He cupped a warm hand around the back of my neck as he kissed me, the touch intimate and exciting. When he released me, it was all I could do not to heave a sigh.

As I stepped back and watched him go, my mind went to the theory of relativity. I'd never studied physics, but I knew Einstein's theory had something to do with time and how quickly it passed. I hoped the time between now and when I saw Newton again would pass at warp speed.

Chapter Seven
Dumped

Back at the station on Monday, Captain Lockhart shared with me all of the information and reports he could get his hands on, including the security camera footage of the men robbing the gun and knife store. I mulled over every detail, reading every report at least five times and reviewing the footage in slow motion to see if I could glean any clue as to how the men might have traveled from Huntsville to Birmingham, where they'd been staying, and where they might be headed next and how. I shared the reports and complete video clip with my father and brothers to see if they spotted anything I hadn't. Like me, they saw nothing that provided any clues about the men.

The state police had looked into all possible modes of transportation the men could have used to escape Huntsville and Birmingham. They didn't show up on security footage from any bus or train stations in the area. Two men traveling individually who bore some resemblance to Billy Wayne Almstead and Trent Bosch showed up on cameras at one of the Birmingham airport's security screening checkpoints. Data from the Transportation Security Administration subsequently confirmed the men were merely lookalikes. The identification offered by the two was determined to be legitimate. They were who they'd claimed to be, and they were not the escaped fugitives.

Because criminals on the lam often stole cars, the investigators looked into all reports of stolen vehicles and car-jackings or attempted car-jackings to date. No luck there, either. It was possible they'd used the cash they'd obtained from the ATMs with the stolen debit cards to buy a prepaid credit card. If so, they could have set up an Uber or Lyft account and gotten a getaway ride from the service in a car operated by an unwitting driver who had no idea they were aiding and abetting criminals. But the state police had been in touch with drivers working in the area around the time of the gun store robbery, and none said they had provided a ride to anyone resembling the escapees.

We were left us with the possibility that the men had hopped a train, obtained a ride from someone who hadn't come forward, or walked the hundred miles from Huntsville to Birmingham without being spotted. The latter seemed unlikely. State police were following up with ex-cons who'd done time in the Limestone facility during the fugitives' tenure, who might know the men and be willing to help them out. So far, though, they'd come up empty.

On Tuesday morning, the rain finally let up in the northern part of the state. As I was writing a speeding ticket to a man who'd been doing 83 in a 65 zone, the thought crossed my mind that, if the men had stolen a vehicle to get from Huntsville to Birmingham, maybe the owner of the vehicle hadn't discovered it missing yet. The owner could be out of town on a trip. Or maybe the owner was an elderly person who spent most of their time in their home and rarely ventured out in their vehicle, maybe someone who lived in a high-rise for retirees and kept their car in an underground garage or parking lot where it wasn't visible from their windows. Farmers and ranchers often kept old trucks and tractors in barns, sometimes with the keys left on the seat for convenience.

When my shift was over late that afternoon, I returned to the precinct and checked in with Captain Lockhart, who had yet to leave for the day. I rapped on his doorframe and he looked up from his desk. "Mind if I do some more poking around? I thought I'd check with the Birmingham PD and see if there were any new reports of stolen vehicles. I might check with Huntsville, too."

"I can't see the harm," he said. "Just be sure to let them know who you are and why you're interested. Nobody can blame you for taking a personal interest in the matter, but we don't want to step on the toes of the state police."

"Yes, sir."

I walked down the hall to room full of cubicles we referred to as the bull pen. I plopped down at a desk, phoned the Birmingham police departments, identified myself, and asked whether there had been any new reports of missing vehicles.

The woman in records said, "We had a couple of reports today. A VW Beetle and a Toyota Highlander."

While the Highlander was a large SUV and could easily accommodate the men and a virtual armory of stolen weapons, they'd have a hard time cramming themselves and the stolen guns and knives into a tiny Beetle. Even so, it was possible. And maybe they'd think we'd be less likely to figure things out if they stole an unlikely getaway car.

"When was the last time the owners saw the vehicles?" I asked.

"The owner of the Highlander said they drove it last night and parked it in their driveway."

"And the VW?"

"Sunday morning, when she took it to get coffee. The owner parked it in the lot at her apartment complex. Came out this afternoon to find it gone. None of the other residents of the complex seem to have seen anything, and there aren't any cameras in the lot."

While I supposed it was possible the men had stolen the SUV or the Beetle, it would mean they'd have had to hide out somewhere with their stolen cache of weapons before taking it. *Where could they have hidden? A seedy motel? A campground? A city or neighborhood park? Inside another vehicle they'd taken?*

I thanked the woman for the information and jotted some notes to add to my research file. I picked up the phone again and dialed the number for the Huntsville Police Department. There, I hit possible pay dirt.

The records clerk on the other end of the line said, "A dump truck was reported missing from a construction site today. They don't know when it was taken. Nobody'd been working there since it started raining last Friday. The operator of the truck admitted he stashed a spare key in a magnetic case under the step beside the driver's door."

In other words, anyone who found the key could have used it to access the truck and drive it away. My body began to tingle. Could the escapees have taken the dump truck? It was an unlikely getaway vehicle, but they'd be desperate. They'd take what they could find.

Construction equipment was a common target for thieves, especially the smaller machines like Bobcats and excavators that weren't intended to be driven on roads and bore no license plates. Companies often put transceivers on the equipment so that it could be located and recovered if stolen. Maybe the truck had such a device, too. "Does the dump truck have a tracking device?"

"Not according to the report," the clerk said.

Dang. The truck's owner probably figured no one would take such a large piece of equipment, especially one with a VIN number and license plate that could be easily traced and matched. "Where was the construction site?"

The clerk rattled off an address and I noted it on my pad. "Thanks."

I ended the call and quickly ran a search on a mapping website to determine the distance between the construction site and the laundromat where the fugitives had stripped out of the scrubs from the prison infirmary and stolen street clothes. The website indicated the two points were two and a half miles apart. On the rideshare bicycles, the fugitives could have made it from the laundromat to the truck in ten minutes, maybe even less. After all, they'd be motivated to get a move on.

I printed out the map and carried it down the hall to show it to the captain. I handed it to him over his desk. "Check this out. The map shows the distance between the laundromat where the fugitives left the nurse's car and the building site where a dump truck was discovered missing today. The truck was last verified to be on the site Friday. With all the rain they've been having in Huntsville, the crew hasn't been working. I'd bet the men ditched the bicycles near the site and took the truck."

Captain Lockhart's head bobbed as he processed the map and the information I'd given him. He turned to his computer, determined which division of the Huntsville PD patrolled the area where the truck had been taken, and picked up his phone to give them a call. After identifying himself he said, "Let me talk to the supervising officer on duty." He held for a few seconds before being transferred. Once he'd explained the situation, he said, "Would you mind sending an officer out to the construction site to see if there are three rideshare bikes lying around?" He paused a moment as the other person spoke. "Great." He provided his phone number, hung up, and returned his attention to me. "I'll give you a call once I hear back."

"Can I wait, instead?" I was impatient to learn whether I was on to something or not. Besides, I'd invested time and energy into the matter. I deserved to be involved.

The captain frowned, but he indulged me. "If you're going to be hanging around my office, you can at least be useful." He reached over to his in-box, picked up a document, and handed it to me. "Check this over for typos."

I looked down. The document was a draft of the captain's weekly precinct report, intended to be submitted to the police chief. I was proud he trusted me with such an important communication.

I pulled a pen from my pocket to mark the page. While it was well-written, direct, and concise, I did find an incorrect word—a suspect was found with "gum" in hand rather than "gun." I also found a transposition error that spell-check hadn't caught, an event that allegedly took place on the fourth of "Yam" rather than "May."

As I handed the edited report back to the captain, his phone rang. He grabbed the receiver and jabbed the button to take the call. "Captain Lockhart." He listened for a moment, his gaze moving from his desk to me, a proud grin spreading across his face. "Take those bicycles into evidence and check them for fingerprints. See if any prints match the fugitives. Also see if any identifying numbers on the bikes match the ones rented with the doctor's credit card." He listened another moment. "Thanks."

Once he was off the phone, he said, "You called it, Officer Rinaldi. The bicycles were found tossed into one of the construction dumpsters. I'd be surprised as hell if the bikes don't match up with the ones the escapees took. I'm going to get in touch with the state police. They'll want to put out a BOLO alert on that dump truck."

I stood, beaming with pride that I'd helped lead them to an important clue, one that, with any luck, could in turn lead us to the fugitives. As I turned to head to the door, the captain said, "Good work, Rinaldi. On both the edits and the truck."

I gave him a smile and a salute. "Thank you, sir."

Chapter Eight
The Truck Stops Here

On the ride home, I pondered the excitement I'd felt on learning that my research had led to something useful. While I enjoyed being a street cop, I had to admit that the little bit of investigating I'd done today was stimulating and rewarding in an entirely different way. I'd never consider giving up my motorcycle to work in police administration, but would I do it to become a detective? It was something to think about.

I was in my kitchen, feeding my furry boys their dinner, when my cell phone pinged. I checked the screen. Sure enough, the state police had sent a be-on-the-lookout alert for the dump truck, informing recipients that it had possibly been stolen by the wanted men. I wondered and worried how far the men might have gotten in the truck. *Could they have made it all the way here to Mobile?* Though it was a small consolation, at least if the men tried to roll up to my place in a big, noisy dump truck, I'd hear them.

#

The next morning, the captain called me with more information. "Prints from all three of the fugitives were found on the rideshare bikes."

Although this particular piece of news was expected, I nonetheless felt a fresh tingle of excitement. *We're closing in on them.* "What about the dump truck? Has it been located?" A big vehicle like that would be hard to hide.

"It was," he said, "about an hour ago and about a half mile from the gun store in Birmingham that the men robbed. It was abandoned in a shopping center parking lot."

I wasn't sure how to feel about that fact. On one hand, finding the truck meant we were on the men's trail. On the other hand, we no longer knew what vehicle, if any, they might be using now. *So close but yet so far.* I ended the call with the captain, hoping news of an arrest would come in soon.

#

Over the ensuing days, photos of Billy Wayne Almstead, Trent Bosch, and Daytona Dickerson appeared repeatedly on television news reports and in print news sources. Billboards featuring images of the three escapees went up beside interstates in the southeast. Flyers were posted in government buildings and in the windows of businesses. A $50,000 reward was offered for information leading to the arrest of the fugitives. The head of the state police held news conferences calling on the public to help in their search. Meanwhile, a close eye was kept on their former associates. If the men came to them for help, they'd be nabbed in a heartbeat.

News came in about the fugitives, but it was not the news I'd been hoping for and it was unclear if any of it was legitimate. Hundreds of people reported having seen the escaped convicts out and about at various locales. Someone claimed to have seen the men at a strip club in Dothan, Alabama. Another claimed the men were in the crowd at the Talladega Superspeedway. Someone alleged they'd seen Dayton Dickerson buying beer and cigarettes at a convenience store in an Atlanta suburb. The three had allegedly been spotted at a roadside motel in Kissimmee, Florida, though when local police went to the motel they found only three men who bore a passing resemblance to the escapees. The fugitives had even been purportedly sighted driving an airboat through the Everglades. Unfortunately, none of the reports panned out and no arrests were made.

Like others, I was left to speculate. Where had the men gone after ditching the dump truck and robbing the gun and knife store? Were they still together, or had they split up? Might they have turned on each other, maybe one of them taking the other two out and dumping their bodies somewhere? It was possible. After all, people in desperate, stressful situations often ended up at each other's throats.

For all we knew, buzzards could be circling their corpses somewhere in the Alabama countryside.

On the bright side, during these days my relationship with Newton flourished. We went to a movie, walked Brillo on the beach, saw a local live band in concert, tried a new Thai restaurant. He was both fun and funny, and I felt myself starting to fall for him.

On a weekend that both Newton and I had free, we decided to drive up to Birmingham to perform our own investigation. Not that we thought we were smarter or better equipped than the state police, but because I had to do something, anything, to feel like progress was being made. Sitting still and doing nothing felt like giving up, like surrender. I didn't like that feeling. I didn't like living in constant fear, either. I preferred to be proactive.

We left Mobile as the sun came up, heading north on Interstate 65. We'd brought some gear with us. Flashlights. Binoculars. Newton had even brought a camera-equipped drone that he could fly over areas to provide us with an aerial view, if needed. I'd never have thought of it. *It pays to be dating a geek.* I'd worn my police uniform, hoping we'd get less pushback and more cooperation from the people we spoke with today.

We stopped at a roadside café along the way for a hearty, if not heart-healthy, southern breakfast. Biscuits and gravy. Grits. Home fries seasoned with sauteed onions and green peppers. *Yum.* Of course, we topped it all off with several cups of coffee.

Fueled by carbs and caffeine, we headed back out on the road. An hour later, we arrived at the gun and knife store the fugitives had burglarized. As we approached the clerk, I noticed he had very short hair, as if it had recently been shaved, as well as a number of wide scars on his scalp and face that were still slightly pink, having yet to fully heal.

"Hi," I said. "I'm Officer Chastity Rinaldi with the Mobile PD." I gestured to Newton. "This is Mr. Isaac, my technical assistant." It was as good a title as any. "I'm guessing from your shaved head and those fresh scars that you're the guy who was attacked by the escaped convicts."

He cut me a sharp look. "That's right. Keep waiting to hear they've been caught, but seems they've outsmarted law enforcement so far."

I tried not to take his harsh assessment personally. I knew the state police were doing their best, but I also couldn't blame him for his anger. In fact, I could relate to it. I was furious, too. Those violent, sick creeps had no right to be part of our world. "I'd like to see the men caught, too. I was the rookie who pulled them over on I-10 and sent them to prison five years ago."

His scowl morphed into a look of curious surprise. "That was you? For real?"

"For real." I pulled back my sleeve to show him the scar left behind where one of the bullets had grazed me. "Luckily for me, they weren't better shots. Of course, you've got me beat in the scars department."

He exhaled a sharp breath. "Can't say I like the scars, but I consider myself lucky, too. They could've killed me." He cocked his head. "I thought the state police were handling the escape."

"They are," I admitted. "But I've got an interest in moving this case along, and I'm finding it hard to just sit still and wait. Right after they were sentenced, Daytona Dickerson told me they'd break out of prison and come for me."

The man's face clouded. "I can see why you'd want to get involved, then. Can't be any fun to sit around wondering if they'll make good on their threat."

"Exactly." I told him that I'd read over all of the reports I could get my hands on, including the statements he'd given to the police. "I also reviewed the security camera footage from here in the store. It was brutal."

"I saw it, too." The man's gaze shifted, looking past me now as if attempting to avoid seeing what was in his mind's eye. "First time I cried since I was a kid."

We stood in silence for a moment until he faced me again and I continued.

"You may have heard that they stole rideshare bikes in Huntsville, and switched them for a dump truck to drive down here to Birmingham. My guess is that, by the time they left here with the weapons, they must've had another vehicle. They'd need space to carry all the weapons they stole."

"They tossed everything into duffle bags," he said, "but they were big duffle bags." He pointed to a display of extra-large black nylon tactical bags. The bags had both short handles and longer shoulder straps that would give a person the option of carrying the bag in a hand at their side or backpack style on their back. If a bag was worn on the back, it would long enough to stretch from above the person's head to below their buttocks. Speculating, he said, "Can't imagine it would've been easy to lug all that weight on foot for long. Think maybe they called an Uber or Lyft?"

While it was possible, it seemed unlikely. They'd realize the driver might identify them as the escaped men, and surely a driver would wonder what types of things the men were carrying in their large duffles. I supposed they could have summoned a ride and then stolen the car from the driver, but no reports of a stolen car—or a missing driver—had come in over the recent weeks. I shared my thoughts with the man. "Has anything new come to you since you last spoke with the state police? Anything at all?"

He shrugged. "I told them everything I remembered. It wasn't much. Everything happened fast and they were only in the store a few seconds before they knocked me out."

"All right." I pulled one of my business cards out of the breast pocket of my uniform and handed it to him. "If something comes to mind, please give me a call. I'd like to see these guys back in prison, for me and you both."

We returned to Newton's Prius, where I released a long, loud sigh. "I don't know what I expected. I mean, it's not like the walls were going to talk to me, share some secret they overheard after the clerk was unconscious." *If only.* The store's security cameras recorded no audio, either. "The odds of the state police overlooking something are small."

"You're the one who figured out the dump truck was a clue, that they might have taken it."

"True, but the state police would have put two and two together eventually, probably sooner rather than later. I just beat them to it."

Newton frowned. "I don't think you're giving yourself enough credit. You're very clever."

"If I'm so clever, why don't I know what to do now?" I closed my eyes to think. When I opened them a moment later, I was none the wiser. "I suppose we could drive around the area, take a look and see if anything catches our eyes, gives us an idea." I pulled out my phone, logged into the mapping app, and searched for the shopping center where the dump truck had been found. I pointed to our right. "Head that way."

Newton started his car and pulled out of the lot. Following my instructions, he executed a few turns. In minutes, we were at the shopping center. The store windows were decorated with flyers asking anyone who'd seen the men to call 9-1-1.

My eyes darted about. Nothing stood out to me. I logged back into the app and pulled up directions to Huntsville. When the automated voice noted our location, Newton cocked his head. "If I knew we'd be driving all the way up to Huntsville, I would've packed a toothbrush."

Chapter Nine
Untitled

"We won't drive all the way to Huntsville," I said. "I just want to see what the men passed on their way into town."

"Got ya."

There were several roads the men could have taken into the city. I-65. Highway 31. Even I-22 or Highway 79 if they'd taken a roundabout route. We decided to drive fifteen miles out on each of them to see what we might see.

As Newton cruised slowly along I-65, I looked for places where a vehicle might have been stolen and the theft remain, as yet, unnoticed. We passed a public storage facility where a number of boats and small RVs were parked, waiting for their owners to return and take them out for recreation. Some of the RVs were trailer style, requiring a vehicle to pull them. But others were the drivable type.

I gestured to the place. "Think maybe the guys stole an RV? Some people buy them but rarely end up using them."

He shrugged. "Could be. But that storage place has a security gate and fence around it. How would they get in?"

I hated to point out the obvious, but . . . "The jail has a fence around it and they still got out."

"Good point," he conceded. He squinted as he eyed the place more closely. "I guess they could've climbed the fence or followed someone in."

I twirled my finger in the air. "Take the next exit and circle back."

He did as I'd asked and, soon thereafter, we turned into the facility. The two of us went inside the cinder block office building, and I spoke with the manager, telling her the reason for my visit. "Can you tell me whether an RV might be missing?"

"Nobody's said anything about an RV that's up and disappeared. But let's go out and take a look." We made our way down the area where boats and RV were parked under an aluminum covering to protect them from the elements. Each spot was numbered. She jotted down the number of each empty spot before leading us back inside. "I'll check the numbers against my records."

For each empty spot, she proceeded to verify either that the space was not currently rented, or that the renter had been by the facility in recent days, as indicated by the security keypad data, meaning they would have discovered if their RV was AWOL. She put her finger on the list she'd jotted down. "There's supposed to be an RV in spot 307. The renters haven't been by in two months."

"What type of RV?" I asked.

"A Winnebago motor home."

In other words, the type of RV someone could drive away and live in. That tingling sensation returned. "Call them, please."

She picked up her phone and dialed their number. She wobbled her head left to right, indicating that it was ringing. When they answered, she said, "Hey. I'm calling from Park-and-Pack mini storage about your RV. Got a police officer here looking into a possible theft. We don't see it in its spot. Wondering if you might be able to tell us where it is." She listened for a moment and then covered the mouthpiece, paraphrasing their response. "They've got it down in Orange Beach for the summer."

Dang! So much for this lead.

The woman waved the receiver. "Anything else you want me to ask them?"

"No. Thanks."

She thanked the person on the line and hung up.

"I appreciate your help," I told her.

Newton and I spent the rest of the day visiting other storage facilities in the area, going through the routine over and over, but coming up empty. I felt defeated and was about to give up and tell Newton to head back to Mobile when an auto repair shop on the side of the highway caught my eye. Several cars were parked in the lot along the road frontage, prices scrawled across their windshields in bright yellow washable glass paint. The windshield of a 2012 Ford Escape read: Low mileage - $5K OBO. An older Hyundai Elantra was offered for $1,300. A rusty 80's era pickup was for sale for a mere $450. A plywood sign leaned against the front bumper of the pickup. The sign read: SHOWCASE YOUR CAR HERE $25/WEEK.

Could the escapees have bought a used car here? I pointed to the place. "Turn in."

It was 5:00 and the mechanics were putting away their tools, calling it a day. I raised a hand in greeting and stepped into the bay. "One of you own this place?"

"I do," said a man in coveralls who was wiping down a greasy wrench with a terrycloth rag. "What's up, officer?"

I hiked a thumb to indicate the cars parked along the edge of his lot. "What kind of records do you keep on the people who park their cars here?"

He snorted, but it was a good-natured snort. "That's a loaded question."

"I'm wondering if someone we're looking for might have bought one of the cars."

The guy motioned for me to follow him into his office. There, he stepped over to a rusty, cockeyed cabinet and opened the top drawer with a *screeeech*. He chuckled. "Suppose I need to get some oil on that." He pulled out a manila file folder covered with greasy fingerprints and plunked it down on his desk. "Those are my records. Have at it."

"Thanks." While I plopped down in the rolling desk chair, Newton scooted over a vinyl seat from the customer waiting area and sat down next to me.

I opened the folder. Inside was a stack of simple, single-page contracts setting out the terms for people wanting to offer their cars for sale on the auto shop's lot. The $25 per week rate was cash only, payable up front, no refunds, no exceptions. Sellers could meet potential buyers on the lot. Use of the lot was at the seller's risk. The owner of the shop was not responsible for any damages or theft. Cars were subject to towing immediately for failure to pre-pay the weekly rental fee. At the bottom of each page was a place for the car's owner to sign and provide their contact information, as well as the make, model, and license plate of the vehicle. Below that the dates of payments were scrawled.

I sorted through the records, pulling out three contracts where the last payment made was for the week that included the dates the men had busted out of prison and robbed the gun and knife store. My assumption was that the contracts ended when the car sold, though it was possible the vehicle's owner might have removed the car from the lot without selling it.

The subject of one of the contracts was a 1997 Mercedes SL500. Having worked traffic detail as long as I had, I knew cars. The model was only a two-seater. Unless one of the men had ridden in the trunk, the car wouldn't accommodate all three of them. And what would they have done with the stolen weapons?

The second contract was for the display of a 2008 Kia Sportage. The smaller SUV would have been able to accommodate both the men and the weapons. I logged into my laptop and ran a search of the DMV records. The data showed that the SUV had transferred ownership two days after the men had robbed the gun store. In other words, the SUV was irrelevant.

The final contract concerned a silver 2004 Dodge minivan. The car would have been plenty big to haul both the men and their arsenal. Still, it was possible someone else had bought the vehicle. I logged into the DMV records. Per my search, the van was still registered in the name that appeared on the auto shop's contract. *Did the owner decide not to sell it, after all, or had the buyer failed to file the paperwork to transfer ownership?*

Newton saw me sit up and raised his brows. "You find something?"

"Maybe." I whipped out my cell phone and placed a call to the number noted on the contract. After identifying myself, I said, "It's my understanding you had parked your minivan at an auto repair shop off Highway 31 and offered it for sale."

"That's right," the woman said. "Is there a problem?"

"I don't know yet," I told her. "Did you happen to sell it?"

"I did," she said. "Didn't get much for it, though. The guy would only pay me seven hundred dollars. I wanted twice that. But I'd had the van up for sale for a while, and I suppose the kids had sort of trashed it. There was magic marker scribbled on the seats and juice stains on the carpet—"

"What guy?" I snapped, my patience gone. "What was his name?"

"I don't recall," the woman said. "Not sure he ever told me. He handed over the cash and I handed over the title."

"He hasn't put the car in his name yet," I told her.

"Really? That's strange."

Or is it? If it was one of the convicts who'd bought the van, it would make sense that he hadn't applied for a title in his name. "What did the guy look like?" I asked.

"Like your average Joe," she said.

But was this average Joe, "Black? White? Latino? Asian?"

"White," she said. "Brown hair. Honestly, I don't remember much about him other than he didn't smell so good. Like he'd been working hard, or maybe skipped a shower."

"Was anyone with him?"

"No," she said. "He was by himself."

"Mind if I swing by and show you some photos, see if you can identify him?"

"I'll be here."

I thanked the owner of the body shop and we drove to the woman's house. Two older teens lounged in the living room, staring slack-jawed at the television, the arrival of a police officer barely registering. No wonder the woman had ditched her minivan. Her children were of driving age themselves now. No need for a mom-mobile.

We took seats around the kitchen table, where I prepared a virtual lineup on my laptop. It included mug shots for all three of the fugitives, as well as mug shots of seven other men we'd arrested in recent years who resembled them. Once I had the pictures in place, I turned my computer so that the screen faced the woman. "Do you see the man who bought your car here?"

Her gaze moved from photo, to photo, to photo, her eyes narrowed as she assessed each one. "I can't swear to it," she said, tapping the screen. "But number five could have been him."

I turned my screen back around and my stomach flip-flopped. Number five was Daytona Dickerson. *We're on their trail!*

The woman eyed me. "Wait. Is he one of those escaped convicts?" Before I could even respond, she gasped, the answer evidently written on my face. "My God! He is, isn't he?" She pointed a finger at my face. "And you're that rookie cop who arrested them! I saw you on the news back then and again recently when they replayed footage from their trial."

I nodded in confirmation. "I need to pass this information on to the state police, let them decide how they want to handle things."

They might want to keep the information quiet, let the men think that law enforcement had no idea that they were driving the van, and try to find them surreptitiously. Or they might want to broadcast the information far and wide, to see if anyone spotted the van. Either way, it wasn't my decision to make.

I placed a quick call to the captain, who in turn called the state police, who in turn sent a pair of investigators to the woman's house to interview her. One was male and one was female, but both had similar short, pewter gray hair and stocky builds.

After the male investigator and I had exchanged introductions, the female detective extended her hand. "I'm Detective Bell."

I took her hand and gave it a firm shake. "Officer Cha-Cha Rinaldi."

The woman who'd sold the car told them the same things she'd told me. She'd dealt with only one man, who'd developed quite a funk. She didn't remember whether he'd mentioned his name. He looked a lot like Daytona Dickerson, but she couldn't be sure whether it was him or not.

Detective Bell said, "If you had to place odds, what would you say the percentage chance was that the man you saw was Daytona Dickerson?"

The woman looked up in thought. "Seventy? Maybe seventy-five?"

The investigators exchanged glances. The male one said, "Not good enough." He cut his gaze to me and the woman. "We can't put this information out and risk some vigilante with a shotgun taking the law into his own hands and potentially injuring or killing a man who may be innocent."

Though I understood their decision and, frankly, believed it was the right one, I was nonetheless frustrated. The car would be located much faster if everyone in the state, law enforcement and civilians alike, were on the lookout for it. With only the police watching for the vehicle, and with police also having to keep an eye out for other lawbreakers, the chances of finding the car quickly, or finding it at all, were much smaller. Still, at least it gave law enforcement something to do, a lead to pursue. *With any luck, we'll find those rotten bastards.*

Detective Bell turned to me. "You're a smart cookie, you know that?"

"Thanks." I felt my chest swell with pride. I'd better keep my ego in check or I'd burst out of my Kevlar vest.

Chapter Ten
Seas the Moment

Unfortunately, though law enforcement throughout the state and southeast were keeping their eyes peeled for the silver Dodge Caravan, no one had spotted it yet. I'd been initially buoyed that I'd uncovered yet another clue that could be critical to the case, but so far it hadn't panned out.

Meanwhile, Newton and I continued to date, spending more and more time together. No matter what we did, I had a good time. We went on a walk through the botanic gardens and Bienville Square. We toured the USS Alabama battleship. We kayaked in the wetlands of Meaher State Park. I accompanied him and his team to a robotics tournament in Atlanta shortly before the school year ended. His team had made some improvements to Geary, and the robot was faster, more maneuverable, and more capable than ever. They placed third in the regional robotics tournament, a best for the team.

The longer the fugitives were on the run, the less I worried about them coming after me. *If seeking revenge on me had been their priority, wouldn't they have attempted it by now?* I ignored the little voice inside me that suggested maybe they were simply waiting for a good opportunity to carry out their threat. But that voice continued to whisper to me, especially in the wee, dark hours of the night when I woke in a cold sweat with my heart pounding so hard in my chest it felt like my ribs were vibrating.

On a Friday in early June, school let out for the summer. Newton and I celebrated by packing up his Prius with beach gear and heading off for a fun vacation in Orange Beach. My mother had driven down to pick up Brill and Knuckles, taking her "grandpets" back to Montgomery to spend the weekend with her and my father. She was the only one I trusted with my precious cat and dog. She doted on them even more than I did, if that was possible.

Newton and I arrived at our beachside hotel, enjoyed a casual outdoor dinner along the ocean, and returned to our hotel, taking seats on the balcony to enjoy the sunset. I'd just settled in when my cell phone came alive with an incoming call. The screen indicated it was Captain Lockhart calling.

I looked over at Newton. "It's my captain." Like the day he'd summoned me to his office weeks before, I realized this could be good news or bad news. Maybe he was calling to tell me that Almstead, Bosch, and Dickerson had been apprehended, hopefully without injury or loss of life to innocent people. *Or maybe he's calling to tell me something else entirely.*

I took a breath to steel myself and tapped the button to take his call. "Hello, Captain."

He pulled no punches. "The fugitives are in Mobile."

My throat closed in terror, as if choked by invisible hands. When I could manage a breath, I squeaked, "Good thing I'm not, then."

"Where are you?"

"Orange Beach. I'm on weekend vacation." One which was very likely now ruined thanks to those bastards. "How do you know they're in Mobile?"

"A postal truck went missing from Birmingham. The mail carrier, too. Nobody realized it until she didn't return at the end of the day. Very little of the mail got delivered, only the first couple of streets on the route. They must have hijacked the truck. The mail carrier and truck were found a few minutes ago in the parking lot of a furniture store."

I gulped. "Is the mail carrier okay?"

"She was manhandled, bound, and gagged, but other than a few scrapes and bruises she'll make a full recovery."

I knew that was a lie. She'd never fully recover from being beaten and fearing for her life. I'd been grazed by bullets that fateful day when I'd pulled over the pickup and trailer, and it wasn't something you soon—or ever—forgot. I'd suffered nightmares for months afterward. Only counseling, time, and over-the-counter sleep meds got me through. I still suffered an occasional nightmare or panic attack thinking back to that day. And at least my ordeal had been over relatively quickly. The mail carrier had been forced to ride around in the truck all day with these men, wondering if, when, and how they might put an end to her life. *I'll send those men back to prison if it's the last thing I do.*

It was a stupid question, but I had to ask it. "She's sure the men were the convicts?"

"She identified them from a photo lineup," he said. "Fingerprints confirmed that all three had been in the truck."

So no chance they were lookalikes.

He continued. "We found the minivan not far from the post office. They must have worried they'd been driving it too long, or somehow figured out that law enforcement was on to it."

"What should I do?" I asked the captain.

"Enjoy your weekend," he said. "You're safer there than you would be here. Does anybody know where you are?"

"Only my parents and a couple of friends."

"You didn't mention anything to your neighbors?"

"No."

"Okay. Don't post any pics on social media. The convicts might be watching your accounts."

I'd never been a fan of living online. I preferred the real world. "I'm not on social media."

"Even better," he said. "We've got officers keeping an eye on your place. If they come around, we'll get them."

I couldn't think of a better way to kick off the summer than with those three escaped criminals being rounded up and sent back to their cells.

When I ended the call and set my phone down, Newton cast me a look of concern. "Those escaped felons made it to Mobile?"

"They did. Hijacked a postal truck."

"Does the captain think they're after you?"

"Enough to put officers on my house. Could be they've forgotten all about me, though. Maybe they plan to take their old route through Mobile and head east on I-10 to Miami." But even as I said it, I didn't believe it. Daytona Dickerson had seemed awfully sincere when he'd said they'd come for me. I took a deep breath and slowly exhaled, trying to calm my nerves.

Newton leaned over from his chair and nuzzled my neck. "If you need a distraction, I'm at your service."

A smile curled my lips as his warm breath on my skin curled my toes. "I'll take you up on that."

#

Newton was as good as his word. He provided me with repeated distractions over the next two days, the two of us testing every law of physics. Momentum. Inertia. Gravity. He showed me Newton's second law of motion, his force equaling my mass and acceleration. We applied Newton's third law of motion, too, each one of our actions giving rise to an equal and opposite reaction.

During the downtimes between distractions, we walked the beach, body-surfed, searched for shells and visited the tidepools. My phone pinged once with an incoming text, but it wasn't the communication from the captain I'd hoped for, telling me the men had been taken into custody. Rather, it was a pic sent by my mother of Brillo and Knuckles curled up on my parents' sofa, napping alongside (in Brillo's case) and atop (in Knuckle's case) my dozing father. *Adorable*, I texted back, glad my pets were away from home and out of danger, too.

When the weekend ended and we climbed into Newton's car on Sunday, I had to swallow hard to clear the lump of emotion from my throat. We were heading back to what could be very grave danger.

On the drive, Newton said, "You're chewing your lip. You're worried. Why don't you stay at my place until the fugitives are rounded up?"

"I don't want to put you at risk. What if they followed me to your place after I left the station and I didn't realize it? I'd never forgive myself if something happened to you."

His jaw flexed, his expression hardening. "And you think *I* could forgive myself if something happened to *you*? To you, this relationship might just be mind-blowing sex, but I happen to have developed some warm and fuzzy feelings for you." His tone was half teasing, half serious.

I cut him a sideways glance. Heck, I'd developed some warm and fuzzy feelings for him, too. He wasn't just a fun guy to be around and nice to look at, but he also exposed me to new ideas and ways of looking at the world, and vice versa. We were learning from each other, growing. I admired him, appreciated the personal financial sacrifices he'd made to be a teacher, as well as the extra time and effort he gave to the robotics club. He'd be one of those special teachers his students would remember years from now, recalling the encouragement he'd given them, the clear and consistent care and concern for their learning and advancement. I sensed he felt the same about me, that he respected the sacrifices I made to serve the community.

I sighed. "I kinda like you, too." We rode on in silence for a minute or two, during which I mulled over my options. Finally, I reached a conclusion. "Will I sound crazy if I say that I want to go back to my house? That I hope the guys come after me there so we can catch them once and for all?"

"You mean you want to serve as bait?"

"In a sense, yes."

"I could see that. It's a little crazy, but not entirely crazy."

"Otherwise," I said, "this standoff of sorts could go on forever. Plus, if they give up on coming after me and simply disappear, I'll be looking over my shoulder for the rest of my life." *Not to mention the horrific things they might do to future trafficking victims.*

"Better to end this, then."

"Exactly."

"Let me come stay with you. Me and Geary."

I barked a laugh. "Geary? Why?"

"That robot can be outfitted to do all sorts of things. We could put a video camera on him and have him patrol your yard. Or equip him with stun guns and hide him in your bushes."

"You might be on to something." After all, the department couldn't assign me a full-time bodyguard without taking an officer off patrol, and I didn't want to put any of my fellow officers in danger. I preferred to handle the escaped felons myself, if possible. Maybe Newton and Geary were the way to do that.

Newton slid me a smile. "What do you say? Will you let me be your nerd in shining armor?"

I gave him a definitive nod. "Let's do it."

Chapter Eleven
Sea Spray

Now that Newton and I had developed a strategy for dealing with the escapees, I called my mother and asked if she could keep Brillo and Knuckles for a few more days.

Of course, she was happy to do it, but she also wanted to know why. She speculated. "It's because those escaped convicts are in Mobile now, isn't it? You're thinking they might pay you a visit."

I wouldn't lie to her. "Yes," I acquiesced. "I don't want to put my fur babies in danger."

"I don't want my human baby to be in danger, either," she said.

"The captain's put eyes on my house," I told her. "I'll be fine." Once again, I only wished I felt as confident as I talked.

"Sleep in your vest," she told me. "Shower in it, too. Don't take it off until those guys are locked up again and the key's been thrown away. You hear me?"

I humored her. "Okay, Mom."

When we arrived back in Mobile, Newton and I made stops at both an electronics store and a hardware store for materials and supplies. Once we'd stocked up, we swung by Newton's house to pick up Geary before driving to my place. Newton owned a house very similar to mine, though his place was slightly bigger, slightly newer, and a few miles farther inland. Together, we lifted the robot into his cargo bay. Newton grabbed his toolbox, as well as optional arms, grips, and wheels the robotics team had tried on the robot before deciding on its final design for their competition purposes.

We kept our eyes peeled as we returned to my place. Two of my fellow officers sat in an unmarked sedan down the block, pretending to read books as if waiting for someone. I knew without a doubt that, like the escaped convicts, they had a virtual arsenal with them. Long and shorter-range rifles. Handguns. Plenty of ammo. The officers would be ready to confront the fugitive felons if they dared to show their ugly mugs.

We stopped at my mailbox, where I collected the envelopes, sales circulars, and the two-way radio the officers had placed there so I could use it to communicate directly with them if necessary.

Newton backed into my driveway, pulling his Prius up next to my Kia in the carport. As quickly as we could, we circled around the back, unloaded Geary, and carried him into the kitchen. As wide as the robot was, it barely fit through the door.

Once we were inside, we closed all of the curtains so no one could see in.

I tested the radio, pushing the talk button. "This is Officer Rinaldi. Can y'all hear me out there?"

Two responses of "affirmative" came back. *Good.* I made sure to turn my police radio on, too, to keep an ear on things happening in our precinct.

Newton and I moved my dinette set out of the kitchen to give us more room to work and maneuver. We set about upgrading Geary from cute and competent high school robotics competitor to a tactical defensive weapon. First, we upgraded his wheels to a larger all-terrain style that would allow him to more effectively move across grass, gravel, and up and down curbs. Next, we reinforced his body with bullet-resistant fiberglass panels, augmenting them with sections cut from an older ballistic vest I'd recently replaced with a trimmer, lighter model. We attached various items to the spinning grippers that served as his three hands. A three-foot length of heavy-duty chain. A combination stun gun and flashlight we'd been charging as we worked. A canister of pepper spray. Newton removed Geary's rainbow wig and spinning globe head, and attached a small, live-streaming camera in its place. He'd been sure to get one that worked well in poorly lit environments.

"What do you think?" I asked Newton as we stepped back to admire our handiwork.

"If you were my student," he said, "I'd give you an A-plus."

I'd have earned it, too. Geary looked like a weapon of war now, nothing like the silly contraption he'd been when we'd carried him into the kitchen a few hours earlier.

It was dark by then, and time to put the robot into position. Before going outside, I notified my surveillance team by radio and we made sure all of the outdoor lights were off so it would be more difficult for anyone who might be spying to tell what we were doing. We rolled the upgraded Geary outside onto the carport, obscuring him behind my garbage and recycling bins.

After going back inside and watching the late news, we went to bed. It was the first time Newton had stayed over at my place, but knowing we could be subject to a surprise attack at any moment took much of the fun out of it.

#

I woke Monday morning after a fitful night's sleep. I'd tossed and turned all night, unable to let down my guard enough to sleep soundly. What's more, it felt strange to sleep in my bed without Knuckles curled up next to me and Brillo at my feet, snorting and snoring as he snoozed. It was nice to wake up next to Newton, though. *I could get used to this.*

After showers, coffee, and a quick bowl of oatmeal, he headed off to his place and I hopped onto my police bike to go to work. As I set off down my street, I noticed a different set of undercover officers in place. I refrained from acknowledging them as I passed, not wanting to give them away, though I hoped they realized how much I appreciated their protecting my place while I was away. The last thing I'd want would be to come home to find the escaped felons hiding inside my house.

The morning was uneventful. At lunchtime, I rode through a drive-thru to pick up a burrito for lunch. I carried it back to the station with me so I could eat it at a desk and check in with the captain.

I went inside and rapped on the doorframe to his office. He looked up and waved me in. As I took a seat in one of his wing chairs, he said, "You look wiped out."

Evidently, I appeared as exhausted as I felt. *Should've put more concealer on those dark circles under my eyes.* "I didn't sleep well."

"Understandable," he said. "Can't be easy to relax when you've got a bullseye on your back."

Gee, when you put it that way . . . "You think Almstead, Bosch, and Dickerson are still in town?"

He jerked his shoulders. "God only knows, Cha-Cha. Those men have kept us guessing. It's too bad they aren't more distinctive. They look like most other southern white men."

It was true. Though the men had tattoos and scars that could be used to definitively identify them, none of the tattoos or scars were on their necks, faces, hands, or forearms. So long as they kept their chests and biceps covered by clothing, nobody would notice Daytona Dickerson's confederate flag tattoo, Billy Wayne Almstead's devil with a pitchfork, or Trent Bosch's ex-girlfriend's name, Amanda, written in a curly script inside a cartoon heart tattooed over his actual organ.

After meeting with the captain and eating my lunch, I set back out on the streets. It was an uneventful day. I wasn't sure whether to be grateful for that fact or not.

#

The rest of the week was equally routine. Nothing out of the ordinary happened on my patrols. Nobody tried to sneak into my house to ambush me when I arrived home. The officers keeping an eye on my house reported nothing of note. By the end of the week, the captain decided the escaped convicts must have skipped town and he relieved my watch. Newton insisted that he continue to sleep over, though I surmised he might be using the fugitive felons as an excuse. *Not that I minded one bit.*

Saturday, I was scheduled to work a swing shift from 5:00 PM to 2:00 AM. It was the worst shift, straddling the daytime and nighttime hours and throwing a person's biorhythms totally out of whack. But all the officers had to rotate through the shift every few weeks. It was only fair.

Not much took place before sundown. I issued a couple of speeding tickets. Responded to a shoplifting call at a convenience store, but the culprit was long gone by the time I arrived. Handled a noise complaint in a neighborhood where a family was hosting a sleepover and pool party for their daughter's sweet sixteen birthday. I advised the guests to take the party inside and wished the birthday girl all the best.

As I headed out of the neighborhood, I turned and aimed for the water, figuring it would be nice to take a drive along the oceanside. The moon reflected off the waves, which crashed softly on the shore. I passed a couple of cars headed in the opposite direction, but there was little traffic out this way this time of night.

As I rolled along, a vehicle approached from behind. Atop the car was a lighted red, white, and blue Domino's Pizza delivery sign. *Who would be delivering a pizza out here?* There weren't any houses around and, at this time of night, nearly all businesses were closed. I supposed it was possible that someone who lived on a boat at one of the marinas might have ordered a pizza.

The car gained on me slowly at first, then with alarming speed. My side mirrors lit up like spotlights as the driver turned on the car's bright-beam headlights, nearly blinding me. I could hear the roar of the car's motor, even through my helmet and over the noise of my motorcycle's engine.

There was nowhere to pull off on the shoulder-less two-lane road, which was flanked with marshland. I cranked back on the accelerator to put some space between me and the vehicle. It was all I could do. *Is the driver drunk? On their phone? Trying to kill me?* When the car sped up to match my pace, I realized it was the latter. *Did the fugitives follow me?*

My heart revved as fast as my motor as I pushed the button to activate my mic and called in my location, asking for backup. "The driver is trying to run me down!"

I accelerated some more. While a motorcycle was more maneuverable on curves, we were on a straight stretch of road and the car behind me had little trouble keeping up.

My side mirrors lit up like spotlights again as the car gained on me, only inches from my back tire now. One tap with the bumper and it could be all over for me.

I swerved into the oncoming lane, hoping the car might inadvertently pass by me, but the car swerved, too, staying right behind me. I swerved back. The car did the same. Whoops came from the car now, deep whoops, men finding it hilarious that they were putting my life in imminent jeopardy. *It has to be the escaped convicts, doesn't it?*

If I'd had any doubt, it was gone the instant I heard one of them holler, "Told you we'd come for you, bitch!"

Holy shit-shit-shit!

The next thing I knew, a bullet took out my left side mirror, the glass exploding into shards that chinked against my helmet. The shot had made hardly a sound, thanks to the silencer the men had stolen from the gun and knife shop. Nobody along the waterfront would hear and report a gunshot. *I'm on my own here.*

A few seconds later, another near-silent shot took out my right mirror, leaving me with no way to see what was happening behind me. The situation was desperate, calling for desperate measures. *But what, exactly?* I wasn't some wild west sharpshooter who could fire accurately over my shoulder. If I turned to aim my gun at the car, I'd lose control of my bike and wipe out. My chances of survival at this speed, especially if the car ran over me, were about equal to my chances of one day walking on the moon. My Taser was useless, too. If I shined my flashlight in their face, it could blind them and they might back off. But I doubted it was bright enough to do the job, and the driver could just avert his eyes and use the yellow lines on the road as a guide.

Thwock! A bullet bit into my back, the pain taking my breath away and causing me to double over across my handlebars. A vest might stop a bullet from penetrating the skin, but that didn't mean it wouldn't still hurt like hell to be hit. Grimacing in agony, I did the only thing I could. I whipped my pepper spray from my belt and released a trail into the air behind me. *PSHHHHH!*

Chapter Twelve
Sailing into the Sunset

The car drove right through the cloud of pepper spray which, judging from the men's response, entered the open windows, coated the windshield, and permeated the A/C system. I heard cursing and coughing as the car slowed behind me.

"Fuck!" *Cough-cough.* "I can't see for shit!" *Cough-cough-cough.*

I took a curve, but the driver, incapacitated by the spray, missed it, the car veering into the marsh with a *SPLASH!* No doubt the crash surprised some turtles, frogs, and fish.

Outgunned and injured, I didn't dare stick around. I headed a half mile farther down the road, switched on my flashing lights, and stopped sideways across the road, blocking the lanes. I didn't want anyone else to unknowingly come upon the armed men. Realizing I'd be a sitting duck on my bike if the escaped cons came my way, I scurried into the marsh grass to hide, my gun at the ready.

I got back on my radio, shrieking for someone to get the other end of the road blocked, too. "It's the fugitives!" I cried. "They fired on me!"

In minutes, a chopper was in the air. Its propellor gave off a *whup-whup-whup*, the wind it stirred up causing the tall marsh grass to sway. A spotlight mounted on the underside of the aircraft swept across the dark swamp as the pilot and officer inside looked down, searching for the men. Another ten minutes and the SWAT team had been mobilized, rolling up the road in their armored vehicle, ready to do battle "Fury Road" style. The captain, dressed in civilian clothes, roared up in his cruiser.

He threw open his passenger door. "Get in here, Cha-Cha!"

He didn't have to ask me twice. I rushed over and all but dove into his vehicle.

We sat in silence, our ears locked on the radio, waiting to hear that the chopper or one of the SWAT team members had nabbed the escapees. While the SWAT officers didn't find my attackers in the waterlogged car, they did find a teenaged pizza delivery boy bound, gagged, and terrified.

The captain raised his radio to his mouth. "Bring him to me."

A SWAT officer untied the boy and drove him to the captain's car in the SWAT truck. We climbed out of the cruiser to speak with him.

After introducing himself, Captain Lockhart gave the boy the third degree. "What happened?"

"I was supposed to deliver an order to a room at the Motel 6," he said. "When I pulled up, the three guys were standing outside the room. I was getting out of the car when one of them walked up to my door and grabbed me. He tossed me in the back and climbed in after me. He put a gun to my head and said he'd kill me if I didn't cooperate." The boy gulped, tears forming in his eyes. "He tied me up while the other two guys climbed in the front and drove off. They kept saying things like 'we'll get that bitch tonight,' and 'she's dead.'" His eyes cut to me, as if he realized I was the bitch they'd been referring to. "They drove up and down the interstate until they saw someone pulled over with a police motorcycle behind them. The cop—" His eyes cut to me again, "I guess that was you, was writing the driver a ticket. They took an exit and circled back around twice until they could follow the motorcycle. Next thing I knew, we were out here in the middle of nowhere and the guy in the front passenger seat pulled out a gun and started shooting and the driver tried to run the motorcycle over." He pointed to me as he addressed the captain. "Then she sprayed tear gas at our car and everyone started coughing and we couldn't see and the driver wiped out. Then they all jumped out and ran off."

"So there was three of them?" the captain asked.

"Yeah."

"What did they look like?"

"They were all white," he said. "Regular sized. Brown hair. That's all I can tell you. I only got a quick look and then they tied me up and shoved me down on the floor."

"Did you catch any of their names?" the captain asked.

"I think one of them called the other Tony," the boy said.

The captain and I exchanged a look. More likely, the named he'd heard had been Daytona, but that wasn't exactly a common name.

"Did they say anything else? Where they might be headed?"

"No," the boy said. "After they crashed my car, the driver just punched back the air bag and said 'we need to get the fuck out of here!'"

"All right," the captain said. "Thanks for the information."

The boy burst into a blubber. "Can I call my mom and go home now?"

The captain put a reassuring hand on his shoulder. "Of course, you can. We'll have one of the officers drive you home, okay?" While the boy pulled his cell phone from his pocket and called his mother, the captain summoned an officer to serve as his chauffer.

Shortly after the boy was driven away, a K-9 team arrived and the dog was dispatched to trail the men. Maybe the dog could do what we mere humans could not, and find the fugitives. They set off into the swamp, the handler's flashlight bobbing as the team slogged through the marsh, heading toward the ocean.

Captain Lockhart and I kept tabs on the search via our radios and his night-vision binoculars. Twenty long minutes later, the dog led his handler to a dock that ran alongside a sizable yacht. The dog stopped at the end of the dock and looked out onto the ocean.

The handler's voice came over the radio. "Hercules has alerted on the water. The men must have jumped in here, or maybe taken a boat and escaped onto the water."

The chopper headed out over the sea now, the spotlight illuminating whitecaps and swells as the search continued, now focused on the ocean.

"Stay where you are," the captain instructed the K-9 handler. "We'll be right there."

The captain started his engine and drove us over to the marina. The docks were dimly lit by lights mounted to poles along the walkways. The chief parked his car and we climbed out, heading down the planks and passing the back end of a large yacht christened the 'Bama Buccaneer, until we were standing next to the handler and his furry German shepherd. Hercules sniffed around my knees. Even though Brillo and Knuckles were staying at my mother's, I'd likely picked up some of their scent and stray hairs on my clothing when I'd sat down on my bed earlier to put on my tactical shoes.

The captain ran his gaze along the yacht next to us. No lights were on inside. He cupped his hands around his mouth and called, "Anyone aboard the Buccaneer?" He moved his hands to the sides of his head, cupping them around his ears now to listen for a response over the sound of the surf. None came. Nonetheless, he called, "Mobile Police coming aboard!" He grabbed a rail with his hand and hoisted a leg over the side, and pulling himself aboard. Once he'd managed to get both legs over, he stood and looked down at the boat's deck. "They've been here."

"They have?" I climbed aboard after him and followed his gaze. A handgun and an empty magazine lay on the deck. It wasn't clear whether the escapees had left the gun behind intentionally or inadvertently dropped it in their haste to get away, but, either way, it told us they'd been on this boat. *Could they still be on it?* Terror ricocheted through me until I realized that, if the men were still on the boat, the K-9 would have found them. Hercules had a very smart snout.

As large as the boat was, it would be expected to have some sort of dinghy aboard for emergency situations, such as a fire in the galley. I glanced around, but no emergency craft was in sight. "Think they took a dinghy from this deck?"

"Could be," the captain said. "Let's get in touch with the owners."

He made his way to the bow of the boat and leaned over the side to snap a photo of the license decal with his phone. He waved for me to follow him back to his cruiser. There, he booted up his laptop and logged into the DMV's boat registration database to get the name of the owner of the boat and their contact information.

Armed with this data, he placed a call to the owner of the yacht. After identifying himself, he said, "Can you tell me whether you've got a dinghy of some sort on your boat?" He paused for a moment. "An eight-foot inflatable, huh? What color?" Another pause. "Does it have oars only or is it equipped with a motor?" Another pause. "I see." He eyed me and made a jerking motion with his hand which, though it looked like an obscene gesture, was meant to indicate that the dinghy had a pull-start motor.

After asking the owner to hold, he shared the information with me, and I relayed it to the officers on site via my radio. "You're looking for a gray dinghy. Eight-footer with a motor."

Returning to the phone call, the captain told the boat's owner what happened. "We're out here right now, looking for the escaped convicts. We believe they've taken off in your inflatable boat. The precinct's K-9 led his handler to your boat and alerted at the end of the dock." He advised the boat owner to keep away for the time being. "You're safer staying away from the area. Besides the missing dinghy, there doesn't appear to be any damage to your yacht." He paused another moment. "Is that so? Well, that just might be lucky for us."

The captain ended the call with the owner of the 'Bama Buccaneer and turned to me, a wicked grin on his face. "The owner of the Buccaneer says the motor on the dinghy's been acting up. Says he'd be surprised if they get far."

I pumped a happy fist, cringing when pain shot out from the bullet's point of impact on my back.

Captain Lockhart got in touch with the Coast Guard and the Marine Division of the Alabama Law Enforcement Agency, referred to as ALEA. They sent out teams in small cutters and planes to look for the men. Captain Lockhart continued to spread the word. County sheriffs' departments mobilized boats and put officers in place along the shore, as did police forces for cities and towns all along the bay and on Dauphin Island to the south. Alerts were sent to the neighboring states of Florida and Mississippi, too.

I hung around for another hour, hoping to hear that dinghy's motor had petered out and that the men had been spotted and captured. Unfortunately, no such report came in.

"Go home, Cha-Cha," the captain told me, his voice gentle. "You're in no shape to keep working tonight."

He was right. I was shaking and shivering just as I had the last time I'd had a run-in with these brutes, when, like tonight, they'd taken shots at me. Unfortunately, as jittery as I was, I was in no shape to be trying to control a motorcycle and, without mirrors, it was in no condition to be ridden anyway. One of the other motorcycle cops came to ride it back to my house for me, while another officer gave me a ride to the minor emergency clinic to have my injury checked out. Though the bullet had fractured one of my back ribs, and the bruise it left looked and hurt like hell, none of my organs was damaged, thank goodness. Once everything healed, I'd be good as new. The doc sent me home with extra-strength pain meds and an ice pack.

I thanked my fellow officer as she dropped me at my home.

"Sure you don't need help getting inside?" she asked.

"I can manage." I did manage, though I moved slowly and stiffly to avoid using my injured back muscle or twerking my fractured rib.

I went inside to find Newton was still up, lounging on my couch as he read a sci-fi novel and chowed down on popcorn.

On seeing me enter, he sat bolt upright. "What happened? Are you all right?"

"The fugitives caught up with me," I told him. "Shot out my mirrors and nearly ran me down." I told him how I'd sprayed their vehicle with pepper spray. "They lost control and crashed into the marsh. They took off on foot through the swamp and stole a rubber boat off a yacht. The police chopper is sweeping the waves, looking for them. The Coast Guard and state are involved, too."

Mouth gaping, Newton stood and stepped over to envelop me in his arms. I grimaced and cried out when his arm brushed the spot on my back where the bullet had impacted my vest.

"You're hurt?"

"My mirrors weren't the only thing that was shot."

"What?!"

I gingerly tugged my shirttail out of the back of my pants and lifted it, showing him the near-black bruise indicating the point of impact. A glance in the wall mirror behind us told me the bruising was continuing to spread.

His eyes wide in shock, Newton said, "Can I do something?"

I nodded and said, "You can hold me." I stepped into his embrace, positioning one of his arms around my shoulders and the other around my waist to avoid putting pressure on my wound. I wrapped my arms around his lower back, buried my face in his chest, and burst into sobs.

He held me for several minutes, letting me cry, not trying to shush me, absorbing both my horror and my tears. Finally, I released him, stepped back, and swiped my forearm across my eyes. "Is there any wine left?"

"We've got a full bottle of pinot grigio."

"That's a start."

Chapter Thirteen
Search and Destroy

Over the next few days, the search for the missing men continued.

A team was sent out to scour Gaillard Island, a 1,300-acre manmade island formed by the Army Corps of Engineers with sand and mud they'd dredged up when the Mobile ship channel had been built in the late 1970's. With the island off-limits to humans, it was possible the men had taken the boat there to hide out. It was also possible that their bodies could have washed ashore there. But all the search group found were various salt grasses and birds, including the once-threatened and now-annoyed brown pelicans, who didn't appreciate people trampling around their nesting grounds.

Law enforcement in ATVs scoured the more remote beaches, looking for evidence of an inflatable dinghy making landfall. None was found. Boats and planes continued to patrol the shoreline.

In mid-June, a shrimp boat made an interesting find when it hauled in its net—the deflated dinghy from the 'Bama Buccaneer sans the motor, which was likely sitting on the ocean floor. The vinyl material on one side of the boat had been shredded with something sharp. An analysis was inconclusive. Some speculated that a shark of some sort had attacked the boat. After all, there were a variety of sharks off the Alabama coast and many fed at night, when the men had been out on the water. If the motor had died on the dinghy, one of the men might have slipped into the water to try to fix it and attracted a shark. Others theorized that the desperate men had turned on each other, using the knives they'd stolen from the store in Birmingham to attack, the blades inadvertently tearing into the rubber raft and sinking it. If they'd gutted or gored one another, and their bodies ended up in the ocean, their blood could have attracted sharks or other fish who'd fed on their corpses. The only ones who knew for sure were the missing men and the creatures of the sea.

At any rate, the fact that the dinghy was discovered far offshore was good enough for the powers that be and the media to conclude that the men had not survived whatever ordeal had befallen them. The captain removed my security detail, deeming it no longer necessary to have eyes on my house 24/7. News reporters and journalists moved on to more immediate and urgent stories, the fugitives-turned-fish-fodder no longer making the headlines.

With the escaped convicts presumed dead, life went back to normal—for most residents of Mobile, Alabama, anyway. But not for me. Until I saw each and every one of the convicts spread out on a marble slab, or at least enough parts of them to prove they were deceased, I wouldn't—*couldn't*—accept that they'd perished at sea.

Newton accepted the science related to the currents in the gulf. The Corriolis Effect, caused by the earth's rotation, resulted in a loop current that could carry objects in a circular pattern. Though it would be fitting for the men's bodies to swirl around the sea as if in a toilet, the Gulf Stream could pull water from the gulf and carry it up the eastern seaboard until it headed northeast to Europe, Iceland, and the British Isles. But, like me, Newton wouldn't be satisfied until he had irrefutable proof that the men had passed on.

"A head, maybe," he said, "or a leg. Hell, I'd even be satisfied with a single hand or foot. I'm not hard to please."

He and Geary continued to bunk with me most nights, though my friends implied he might be playing along with my fears simply because I found sex to be a great stress reliever and he was enjoying a steady supply of physical satisfaction. Though I was irritated by their dismissiveness of my concerns, I knew their hearts were in the right place. They didn't like to see me worried and obsessed, constantly looking over my shoulder. They wanted me to be able to live my life without the specter of imminent and violent death hanging over me.

Having missed Brillo and Knuckles terribly, I drove to Montgomery and brought them back home. I only hoped I wasn't putting my precious pets in danger.

While I worked the morning of the Independence Day parade, riding ahead to ensure the path was clear for the floats, marchers, and performers, I was lucky enough to have the evening off. Dealing with drunks shooting off both illegal fireworks and their mouths wasn't much fun, as I'd learned in previous years.

Newton and I found a quiet spot along the beach where we could watch the fireworks without getting tangled up in the traffic and crowds. We kicked off our shoes and spread a blanket out on the sand so we could lie on our backs and best enjoy the show. As we waited for the fireworks to begin, my nerves were soothed by the *shush-shush-shush* of the soft surf sliding ashore and slipping back into the sea.

Newton reached over and took my hand in his, bringing it to his lips. He gave the back of my hand a gentle kiss before setting it back down on the blanket, but he didn't release it. "I got an e-mail from Tamika today. She landed a five-grand scholarship for Auburn. She said they were impressed by her involvement with the robotics club."

"That's wonderful!" I knew she'd been one of his favorite students, a hard worker who aspired to a career in electrical engineering. "You must be very proud."

"I am," Newton said. "That girl will go far. She's smart and she's got good leadership skills. She wasn't afraid to ask questions. The other kids looked up to her. I'll miss having her on the team, but I'm curious to see which of my rising seniors will step up and assume leadership roles now. Every year when some of the team members graduate, it changes the dynamics."

"You don't assign their roles?"

"Nope," he said. "It's important for the team-building process and their personal growth for them to work it out for themselves. I just facilitate and suggest solutions if needed so everyone gets heard."

The conversation had me thinking once again of Billy Wayne Almstead, Trent Bosch, and Daytona Dickerson. Given that Daytona had been driving the pickup the day I'd pulled them over five years before, I'd assumed he was the ringleader of their sick circus. I wondered if he was the one driving the car that tried to run me down a few weeks earlier, too. Or might he be the one who'd shot me this time? The mere thought drew my focus to the still-sore spot on my back. Though the bruise had faded from black, to blue, to green, to yellow, it had yet to entirely disappear and the skin could still be sensitive.

I sat up and gazed out at the black ocean. Lights bobbed here and there where people on boats had dropped anchor to watch the fireworks. With any luck, maybe one of them would find the fugitives floating in the water tonight so that I could finally put those men out of my mind and move on. My worry that they'd return to finish me off was like an emotional anchor, holding me in place. Pull as I might, I couldn't seem to lift it.

Newton sat up, too, seeming to sense my turmoil. "Their bodies have to turn up sometime."

While I knew he was only trying to help, his optimism seemed shallow and a little annoying. I cut him a look. "None of the people on that Malaysian plane that went missing have ever surfaced. People have fallen off cruise ships and never been found. Nobody knows what happened to Amelia Earhart."

"Point taken." He exhaled a long, sharp breath. "You know, when my students can't figure something out, I tell them to look at the problem from another angle."

"What other angle is there to this problem?"

"We could pretend to be the convicts, think of things from their perspective. If we were them, and we wanted to come after you, how would we do it? What way would be the easiest?"

I frowned. "You want me to imagine how I might kill me if I were them?" *There's a happy thought.*

He lifted a shoulder. "It's just an exercise."

Off in the distance came the whistling scream of fireworks as a yellow rocket streaked toward the sky, followed by the *pop-pop-pop* of black cat firecrackers exploding. Even after the professional fireworks show was over, these sounds would continue into the night. If I knew I'd be making noise as I committed a crime, tonight would be the perfect night to do it. The sound of the fireworks would provide cover.

A sick feeling slithered into my gut and coiled there. I turned to Newton. "If I were going to kill me, I'd break into my house tonight. I'd wait until some fireworks were popping to cover the noise of me prying a door open or breaking a window. Maybe I'd even have one of my cohorts set off some fireworks nearby to help obscure the sounds I'd make."

"Whoa. You think they're coming tonight?"

"If they're still alive, I do."

He gave my hand a squeeze. "Then we'll be ready for them."

Chapter Fourteen
Firecracking the Case

We stayed to watch the professional fireworks show, oohing and aahing along with the others on the beach. When it was over, we drove back to my house. Brillo and Knuckles met us at the door. Newton took a moment or two in the carport to ensure Geary was fully charged, armed, and ready for action before coming inside and locking the door behind him.

We snuggled up on the sofa with glasses of wine, the dog, and the cat, and watched a rom-com, the perfect midsummer night movie. A little after midnight, we went to bed. *Pops, bangs, whizzes,* and *screes* could still be heard, some in the distance, some sounding as if they were only a street or two away. Brillo didn't like the loud, unusual sounds. He grunted and whined and sighed, before repeating the mantra over again. Finally, he shoved his head under the pillow to block the irritating noises and fell asleep. At the foot of the bed, Knuckles drifted off, too. So did Newton and I, though reluctantly.

A few minutes after 3:00, more popping noises woke me. They sounded as if they were about a half mile away—not in the immediate vicinity where they might encourage neighbors to peek outside, but close enough to obscure the sounds of someone breaking into my house. Brillo raised his head, his ears perked. He made a soft questioning sound—*arrur?*— as if asking whether I'd heard what he had.

I sat up and looked out into the living room. As I did, one of the motion sensor lights out front was triggered and turned on, the glow visible around the edges of the closed blinds. I grabbed my loaded gun from the nightstand and elbowed Newton. He scrubbed a hand over his face and sat up, groggy.

"They're here," I whispered, pointing at the thin line of light around the living room blinds. "Either that, or there's a raccoon in the yard." I'd feel really stupid if it was the latter, but I doubted such was the case.

I could tell by the look on Newton's face that he felt the same way I did. Both terrified and determined. He grabbed his phone from the night table and logged into the app that was linked to the robot's camera. He pushed some buttons to activate the feed. An instant later, the phone's screen illuminated with the image of our cars in my driveway. He placed the phone on the table where he could keep eyes on the screen and grabbed his weapon—Geary's remote control. He moved the joystick in his hand, rolling Geary forward.

Geary moved quietly and effortlessly between our vehicles, stopping at the back bumper of Newton's Prius. Newton turned the robot and the camera swept the yard. Though I'd fully expected to see the escaped fugitives, I still gasped when the camera provided us with a shadowy image of Daytona Dickerson crouching in the bushes below my living room window, a long-barreled rifle in his hands. We saw the back of Billy Wayne Almstead as he circled around the side of my house. A moment later, his shadow passed my bedroom window. They'd devised a clever plan to trap me. With one at the front of my house and another in the back, they could catch me any way I tried to run.

Another round of black cat fireworks went off in the near distance. *Pop-pop-pop!* As if on cue, Dickerson raise the rifle, the butt aimed at the window. But before he could break the glass, Geary rolled toward him, swinging the length of heavy-gage chain.

Dickerson turned toward the robot and stood stock still for a moment, trying to process what he was seeing. Of all the things he might have anticipated, a robot ready for a rumble didn't appear to be one of them. His mouth formed the words *What the fuck?* He seemed unsure what to do. Was he better off in the bushes, which might provide some protection, or should he try to run?

He seemed unable to make up his mind, but that didn't matter. Just as they'd devised tactics to get me no matter how I might respond,

Geary could get him either way he went. Newton used the controller to raise the robot's arm, the chain swinging at the man's waist level now. Geary rolled into the bushes, the chain taking out leaves and limbs, sending up a spray of foliage. I'd have to replace the bushes, but it was a small price to pay for getting to live. I'd never much liked those bushes anyway.

Though the glass of the living room window, we heard Dickerson cry out as Geary worked his way through the protective foliage and landed his first swipe of steel on Dickerson's right hip and glute. "Aaaah!"

That had to hurt like hell. Good. I normally abhorred violence, but sometimes you had no choice but to fight fire with fire.

I jumped on my police radio and called for officers to assist. "The fugitives are in my yard!" I cried. "They've got guns!"

Officer Stassney, as well as several other officers, replied. "On our way."

Dickerson staggered out from the bushes, limping. He raised his rifle and took a shot at Geary. *Blam!* We could see the muzzle flash on the camera. More popping noises sounded in the distance. If anyone had heard the gunshot, they'd think it was merely a firecracker.

His first shot proving ineffective, Dickerson took another shot at the robot. Like the one before, it had bounced off the bullet-resistant panels and Kevlar vest attachment. *Geary wouldn't go down easy.*

Newton pushed a button on the remote and the robot swung the chain again, whacking Dickerson in the ass as he turned to run. The pain was too much. It took him down to the ground, much as I'd taken him down with a knee to the nards years before.

Newton maneuvered the robot until the machine faced the fugitive head on. He glanced over at me, his jaw flexing with rage. "A few more swings of the chain and I could end this guy." He raised his brows in question.

As much as Daytona Dickerson didn't deserve to live after nearly taking my life and shattering those of the women he'd kidnapped, I wanted the pleasure of seeing this man returned to prison. I also didn't want his blood and gore all over my yard. *Ew.* "Shock him instead."

"Anything you say, babe."

Newton rotated Geary so that the arm with the combination flashlight and stun gun now faced Dickerson. The arm stretched out and pressed the device against Dickerson's neck. A bright, flickering lightning bolt quivered between the device and the man's skin. Dickerson shrieked once, then jerked and shimmied like a marionette going through detox. After a few seconds, he fell over sideways.

"Good work," I instructed Newton. "He's down for the count."

Newton pulled the robot's arm back.

Geary's camera gave us an image of Almstead careening around the side of the house. Whether he'd been drawn by his cohort's cry or the smell of his skin sizzling, I wasn't sure. But, either way, he was Geary's target now.

I barked a laugh as the video feed showed Almstead, too, freezing as he tried to process the mechanical being rushing at him, swinging a chain. He backed up too late and Geary landed a solid swipe to his calf. Almstead grabbed his leg and sent up a howl of pain we could hear inside the house. Brillo howled along with him, raising his nose to join in. *Arooo!*

As Almstead attempted to amble way, Geary followed, reaching his robot arm up to zap the man in the ass with the stun gun. Almstead quivered and jerked, uncontrollably twerking. After a few seconds and 25,000 volts, he melted to the ground.

Pop-pop-pop!

The fireworks sounded much closer. We soon learned why. Trent Bosch pulled up in a piece-of-shit Chevy that had seen much better days. No doubt it was another cheap car they'd bought for cash, still registered in the name of its former owner. Before spotting his cohorts on the ground, he tossed a lit pack of black cat fireworks out of the window. We could see the flashes of light on the camera and hear the popping out in my front yard. *POP-POP-POP-POP-POP!*

A moment later, Bosch spotted the two men lying disabled in my yard, attempting to rise. He leaped from the car, leaving the driver's door open behind him. He ran over to Almstead, who was closer to him. Big mistake, as Geary was closer, too. At Newton's command, Geary turned on the flashlight, blinding Bosch, before rolling forward and applying the stun gun to the man's groin. Bosch folded and flailed on the ground.

I raised my nose and pretended to sniff the air. "Is that roasted nuts I smell?"

The street suddenly filled with flashing lights and sirens. My backup had arrived. Lest the robot move and be beaten into scrap metal, Newton lay Geary's remote control down on the table. We continued to watch the feed as my fellow officers easily shackled the escaped convicts.

I picked up my radio. "This is Officer Rinaldi. I'm inside. Safe." *Thanks to the man beside me.* I set my radio down and turned to Newton, tears of relief welling up in my eyes. "I owe you my life."

"Aw, shucks," he said. "I only did what any extraordinarily sexy physicist would do."

I gave him a kiss, grabbed his arm to pull him along behind me, and led him to my front door. I threw it open to face the three fugitives, who'd been hauled to their knees. All of them glared at me, their eyes glowing with rage. I leaned casually against the door jamb, crossed my hands over my chest, and shook my head. "Promises, promises."

Chapter Fifteen
Promotion

With the men being treated for their injuries at a local hospital, shackled to their beds and under the watchful eye of two armed guards each, I could finally relax. They'd never come for me again.

Over the next few weeks, the men were tried for their prison break, their assaults on the prison infirmary staff and the clerk at the gun store, and their attempts to kill me. They received another life sentence without the possibility of parole, this one to be served consecutively after their current sentence, meaning they were up shit creek without a paddle and would die in prison.

The next school year began, and Newton once again served as faculty advisor for the school's robotics club. Geary was allowed to retire, though he was awarded an honorary police badge for his heroic efforts in my front yard. Newton put him on display in his classroom. The robot was an inspiration to teens aspiring to become engineers or physicists, and to those aspiring to a career in law enforcement, as well.

I was out patrolling on my police motorcycle one September afternoon, when dispatch once again summoned me to the captain's office. *Uh-oh.* The last time he'd called me in, he'd dropped a bombshell on me. *What does he want with me this time?*

I returned to the precinct, noting a state police cruiser in the lot. I parked my bike and climbed off, removing my helmet as I went inside. I headed down the hall to the captain's office to find him seated behind his desk. Sitting in one of his wing chairs was the female state police detective I'd met after I'd figured out the fugitives might have bought the used minivan. She stood to greet me.

I gave the captain a nod and extended my hand to the woman. "Nice to see you again, Detective Bell."

"Nice to see you, too, Officer Rinaldi." She held out a hand, inviting me to take a seat in the other chair.

The captain saw the puzzled look on my face and filled in the blanks. "The detective wants to steal you."

"Excuse me?"

The woman chuckled. "Only if you're willing to be stolen. We were quite impressed with the work you did hunting down the fugitives. You figured out not only that they'd stolen the dump truck, but also that they'd bought the Dodge. That took some clever thinking."

A proud blush warmed my cheeks.

"How would you like to work for the Alabama Bureau of Investigation?"

I looked from her to the captain, who beamed with pride as well. "Can I ride a motorcycle?"

She laughed. "Not on the job," she said, "but we'll pay you enough that you can buy a nice bike to ride on your personal time."

I could live with that. I looked back to the captain. "You okay with losing me?"

"To the A.B.I.?" he said. "Sure."

I stuck out my hand to give hers another shake, and sent her a smile. "When do I start?"

*** *The End* ***

About the Author

Photo credit Kyle Cavener

Diane Kelly is a former assistant state attorney general and tax advisor who spent much of her career fighting, or inadvertently working for, white-collar criminals. When she realized her experiences made great fodder for novels, her fingers hit the keyboard and thus began her Death & Taxes white-collar crime series. A proud graduate of her hometown's Citizens Police Academy, Diane is also the author of the Paw Enforcement K-9 series and the Busted motorcycle cop series. Her other series include the House Flipper cozy mystery series, the Southern Homebrew Moonshine series (launching in 2021), and the Mountain Lodge series (also launching in 2021). Diane also writes romance and light contemporary fantasy stories. You can find Diane online at www.dianekelly.com, on her author page on Facebook, and on Twitter and Instagram at @DianeKellyBooks.

***

Dear Reader,

Thanks so much for buying this book! I hope you enjoyed this story as much as I enjoyed writing it for you.

What did you think? Posting a review on Amazon and Goodreads is a great way to share your thoughts with fellow readers and help each other find books you'll love.

Let's connect! Be the first to hear about upcoming releases, discounts, and subscriber-only specials by signing up for my newsletter at NEWSLETTER SIGN-UP. Find me online at my WEBSITE and on my author page on FACEBOOK. I'd love to connect with you on TWITTER and INSTAGRAM, too! And be sure to follow my page on BOOKBUB!

I love to have virtual visits with book clubs! Contact me via my website if you'd like to arrange a virtual visit with your group.

Below is a comprehensive list of my books, as well as excerpts to help you decide if one of them might be next on your to-be-read list.

Happy reading! See you in the next story.

Diane

BOOKS BY DIANE KELLY

The Busted series:
Busted
Another Big Bust
Busting Out

The House Flipper series:
Dead as a Door Knocker
Dead in the Doorway
Murder with a View (coming Feb. 9, 2021)

The Paw Enforcement series:
Paw Enforcement

Paw and Order
Laying Down the Paw
Against the Paw
Above the Paw
Enforcing the Paw
The Long Paw of the Law
Paw of the Jungle
Bending the Paw

The Tara Holloway Death & Taxes series:
Death, Taxes, and a French Manicure
Death, Taxes, and a Skinny No-Whip Latte
Death, Taxes, and Extra-Hold Hairspray
Death, Taxes, and Peach Sangria
Death, Taxes, and Hot Pink Leg Warmers
Death, Taxes, and Green Tea Ice Cream
Death, Taxes, and Silver Spurs
Death, Taxes, and Cheap Sunglasses
Death, Taxes, and a Chocolate Cannoli
Death, Taxes, and a Satin Garter
Death, Taxes, and Sweet Potato Fries
Death, Taxes, and a Shotgun Wedding

Single Title Romances and Romance Novellas:
Love, Luck, and Little Green Men
A Sappy Love Story
One Magical Night
Wrong Address, Right Guy
Love Unleashed

Look for Diane's new Southern Homebrew Moonshine series and her Mountain Lodge series debuting in 2021!

Bending the Paw - Excerpt

Chapter One
St. Valentine's Day Massacre

The Slasher

He reached over to the wooden block of serrated steak knives on the kitchen counter and yanked one out, clutching it in his fist. He slashed and slashed, and the blood splashed and splashed. Over the wall. Over the countertops. Over the floor. Over skin and clothing and shoes.

When he finished his bloody business, a little brown face looked up at him from the doorway. The French bulldog's eyes went wide as she tilted her head in question, wondering about the strange events taking place in the kitchen of her home. She issued a soft whine. He tucked the thick roll of bills into his jacket pocket, zipped the pocket closed to keep the cash secure, and reached down to give the dog a quick pat on the head. "Don't worry, girl. Everything's going to be all right."

Chapter Two
Home is Where the Heart Stops

Fort Worth Police Officer Megan Luz

"What do you say, Megan? Shall we form a pack?" Seth, my hunky, blond, and broad-shouldered firefighter boyfriend was down on one knee in the foyer outside the police chief's office, the place where we'd first met. Our K-9 partners, Brigit and Blast, sat beside him. Brigit was an enormous German shepherd mix with an abundance of fur and even more attitude. Blast, on the other hand, was a sweet, submissive yellow Labrador. All three gazed anxiously at me, Brigit and Blast with big brown eyes, Seth with sexy green ones.

"Yes!" I burst into happy tears as Seth leaned forward and slipped the beautiful brushed gold ring on my finger. It fit perfectly. The round diamond glittered in the dim after-hours light.

As he rose from the floor, I rose from my chair. We wrapped our arms around each other and held tight for a long moment, our chests pressed together, our hearts beating in syncopated rhythm. Appropriate, given that it was Valentine's Day, a holiday in which hearts factored heavily. Not wanting to be left out of our love-fest, the dogs nudged our knees with their noses, trying to force their way between us.

I released Seth and wiped my eyes with my fingers, unable to stop smiling. I glanced at my watch. 9:15. My mom and dad would still be up. "Let's go tell my parents."

"They're not out celebrating Valentine's Day?"

"They've been married forever, and Mom's got classes in the morning. They probably got each other a card and ordered a pizza." Despite having conceived five children, my parents weren't exactly romantic, at least not in the traditional sense. They were too busy for poetry and picnics in the park, and too budget-constrained to splurge on expensive gifts for each other. Theirs was a solid but practical kind of love, expressed through laundry services, lawns mowed, and laughs shared.

Seth eyed me. "Think we'll take each other for granted like that someday?"

I slid him a smile. "If we're lucky."

We made our way to the elevator, rode down to the ground floor, and headed out to the parking lot, where we loaded our furry partners into his seventies-era blue Nova with orange flames down the sides. We aimed for my parents' house in Arlington Heights, an older neighborhood in Fort Worth where both I and popular folk singer John Denver had graduated from high school, though he'd proceeded me by approximately five decades and had later escaped the brutal Texas summers by moving to Colorado. My parents' three-bedroom, two-bath wood-frame house could use a fresh coat of paint, but no matter how many times my father looked at the house and commented that he needed to go to the hardware store for painting supplies, he always forgot about the task once he'd crossed the threshold.

I used my key to unlock the front door, and Brigit and Blast trotted in ahead of us humans. As usual, they headed straight for the kitchen, hoping to steal what remained in the bowl of kitty kibble my mother maintained for her three indistinguishable orange tabby cats.

The dogs having cued a greeting, my dad appeared in the kitchen doorway. Thanks to his Latino heritage, my father had dark hair and warm brown skin, both of which he'd passed on to me. Thanks to time, his hair bore some silver streaks, more with each passing year. "Hey, you two," he said. "There's leftover pizza if you want any."

Seth and I exchanged a knowing glance.

"Thanks," I said. "But we've already eaten."

We entered the kitchen to find the dogs with their heads shoved into the cat bowl, and my mother and my sister Gabby at the table with their homework spread out in front of them. Gabby clutched a handful of her dark hair as she struggled with pre-calculus. My red-haired, Irish-American mother was elbow deep in books on the Great Depression, working on a history paper for one of her college courses. She'd recently returned to school after taking a break of nearly three decades. She was living proof that it's never too late to achieve your dreams and go after your goals.

While the two still had a way to go on their schoolwork, they'd made quick work of a large heart-shaped box of chocolates. Only three of the pieces remained, and two of those had small bites taken out of them. Rejects.

I reached out with my left hand, turning it to and fro to catch the light from the fixture over the table, and grabbed the last remaining intact piece of chocolate. Neither my mother nor my sister noticed my ring. *Good thing they aren't aspiring detectives.* I took a bite of the candy. *Dark chocolate-covered coconut. Yum!* I eyed my sister. "Is this candy from T.J.?"

"Don't ever mention that name again!" Gabby broke down into a blubbering mass and bolted from the room.

Apparently, my question had been a wrong one to ask. I looked to my mother for answers.

"Gabby and T.J. broke up today," she said. "He met some girl at a debate tournament and called things off."

So my little sister had been dumped, not only on Valentine's Day, but also on the day I'd gotten engaged. *Talk about bad timing.* "I'll go talk to her." I turned to Seth. "I'll be back in a minute."
Dad pulled open the fridge door. "That'll give us guys a chance to have a beer." He retrieved a couple of bottles of Shiner Bock and handed one to Seth.

I walked down the hall to the room Gabby and I had shared before I left for college. I rapped softly on the door. "Can I come in, Gabs?"

"Only if you promise not to tell me there's more fish in the sea!"

Busted – Excerpt

Chapter One – Ready, Aim, Fire.

He's coming.

The far-off drone of a high-performance motorcycle engine drifted up the two-lane highway on the warm, early September north Texas breeze, the volume and pitch escalating as the bike grew closer. I had no idea who rode the Ninja, but I'd had my eye on him for weeks.

Today I'm going to nail him.

Sitting on my Harley-Davidson, I dug the heels of my knee-high black leather boots into the loose mix of dirt, gravel, and cigarette butts edging the highway. I eased the machine back from the shoulder until I was fully obscured by the faded yellow sign that read "Welcome to Jacksburg—Population 8,476 Friendly People," under which "and a couple of assholes" had been added in thick red marker, probably by last year's senior class from the rival high school in Hockerville.

Dressed head-to-toe in dark colors, I'd be difficult to spot. A couple of overgrown oleander bushes with pink flowers flanked the sign, providing extra cover. The guy would never see me lying in wait, gun in hand. He wouldn't know what hit him until it was too late. *Heh-heh.* I grasped the gun tightly, resting the grip across my right thigh, grown noticeably thicker over the last few months. *Gah. Time to hit the treadmill.* Craning my neck, I peeked between the swaying limbs of the bush, my gaze locked on the small rise a half mile up the road. A few strands of my dark hair pulled free from my long braid and blew in the breeze, tickling my freckled cheeks. Some might refer to the reddish streaks in my hair as highlights, but the coppery tones were unintentional, the result of wind and sun damage. Mother Nature was my hairdresser now. She was much less expensive than the stylist who'd coiffed my hair when I'd lived in Dallas.

The motor grew louder and my breathing ceased, every muscle in my body locked in place. I was a sniper, waiting for my target. Waiting . . . Waiting . . .

And there he was.

The golden-yellow and black Ninja ZX-14R popped up over the hill, the noise from its powerful engine now a full-blown primal scream, its rider hunched forward over the sport bike like a jockey over a racehorse to maximize aerodynamics. I raised the gun with two shaky hands, resting my forearms on the platform of my double-D breasts. Leveling the barrel, I sighted, squinting through my tinted goggles, and whispered, "One . . . two . . . three."

I pulled the trigger. *Crud.* The display on the ancient radar gun read 729 miles per hour. A Ninja can haul ass, but it wasn't a frickin' rocket. I yanked the gun's power plug out of the bike's cigarette lighter, reinserted it, and tried again. By this time, the Ninja was right on me. I took aim, squeezed the trigger a second time, and checked the readout. 56 mph. Nine miles under the speed limit. *Damn.* Looked like I'd never find out who rode that kick-ass bike.

The motorcycle roared past, kicking up a dusty, warm wind, its rider decked out in a sporty jumpsuit of yellow and black coordinated to match the bike. A quarter mile down the road, the bike turned left onto Main Street, disappearing into the distance and into my dreams.

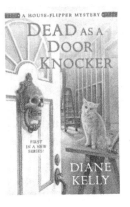

Dead as a Door Knocker – Excerpt

Chapter One
Deadbeats

Whitney Whitaker

I grabbed my purse, my tool belt, and the bright yellow hardhat I'd
adorned with a chain of daisy decals. I gave my cat a kiss on the
head. "Bye-bye, Sawdust." Looking into his baby blue eyes, I
pointed a finger at him. "Be a good boy while mommy's at work,
okay?"

The cat swiped at my finger with a paw the color of pine shavings.
Given that my eyes and hair were the same shade as his, I could be
taken for his mother if not for the fact that we were entirely different
species. I'd adopted the furry runt after his mother, a stray, had given
birth to him and two siblings in my uncle's barn. My cousins, Buck
and Owen, had taken in the other two kittens, and my aunt and uncle
gave the wayward mama cat a comfy home in their hilltop cabin on
the Kentucky border.

After stepping outside, I turned around to lock the French doors that
served as the entrance to my humble home. The place sat in my
parents' backyard, on the far side of their kidney-shaped pool. In its
former life, it had served as a combination pool house and garden
shed. With the help of the contractors I'd befriended on my jobs, I'd
converted the structure into a cozy guest house—the guest being

yours truly. It had already been outfitted with a small three-quarter bath, so all we'd had to do was add a closet and kitchenette.

Furnishing a hundred and fifty square feet had been easy. There was room for only the bare essentials—a couple of bar stools at the kitchen counter, a twin bed and dresser, and a recliner that served as both a comfortable reading chair and a scratching post for Sawdust. Heaven forbid my sweet-but-spoiled cat sharpen his claws on the sisal post I'd bought him at the pet supply store. At least he enjoyed his carpet-covered cat tree. I'd positioned it by one of the windows that flanked the French doors. He passed his days on the highest perch, watching birds flitter about the birdhouses and feeders situated about the backyard.

At twenty-eight, I probably should've ventured farther from my parents' home by now. But the arrangement suited me and my parents just fine. They were constantly jetting off to Paris or Rome or some exotic locale I couldn't pronounce or find on a map if my life depended on it. Living here allowed me to keep an eye on their house and dog while they traveled, but the fact that we shared no walls gave us all some privacy. The arrangement also allowed me to sock away quite a bit of my earnings in savings. Soon, I'd be able to buy a house of my own. Not here in the Green Hills neighborhood, where real estate garnered a pretty penny. But maybe in one of the more affordable Nashville suburbs. While many young girls dreamed of beaded wedding gowns or palomino ponies, I'd dreamed of custom cabinets and and built-in bookshelves.

After locking the door, I turned to find my mother and her black-and-white Boston terrier, Yin-Yang, puttering around the backyard. Like me, Mom was blond, though she now needed the help of her hairdresser to keep the stray grays at bay. Like Yin-Yang, Mom was petite, standing only five feet three inches. Mom was still in her pink bathrobe, a steaming mug of coffee in her hand. While she helped with billing at my dad's otolaryngology practice, she normally went in late and left early. Her part-time schedule allowed her to avoid traffic, gave her time take care of things around the house and spend time with her precious pooch.

"Good morning!" I called.

My mother returned the sentiment, while Yin-Yang raised her two-tone head and replied with a cheerful *Arf-arf!* The bark scared off a trio of finches who'd been indulging in a breakfast of assorted seeds at a nearby feeder.

Mom stepped over, the dog trotting along with her, staring up at me with its adorable little bug eyes. "You're off early," Mom said, a hint of question in her voice.

No sense telling her I was on my way to an eviction. She already thought my job was beneath me. She assumed working as a property manager involved constantly dealing with deadbeats and clogged toilets. Truth be told, much of my job did involve delinquent tenants or backed-up plumbing. But there was much more to it than that. Helping landlords turn rundown real estate into attractive residences, helping hopeful tenants locate the perfect place for their particular needs, making sure everything ran smoothly for everyone involved. I considered myself to be in the homemaking business. But rather than try, for the umpteenth time, to explain myself, I simply said, "I've got a busy day."

Mom tilted her head. "Too busy to study for your real estate exam?"

I fought the urge to groan. As irritating as my mother could be, she only wanted the best for me. Problem was, we didn't agree on what the best was. Instead of starting an argument I said, "Don't worry. The test isn't for another couple of weeks. I've still got plenty of time."

"Okay," she acquiesced, the two syllables soaked in skepticism. "Have a good day, sweetie." At least those five words sounded sincere.

"You, too, Mom." I reached down and ruffled the dog's ears. "Bye, girl."

I made my way to the picket fence that enclosed the backyard and let myself out of the gate and onto the driveway. After tossing my hard hat and tool belt into the passenger seat of my red Honda CR-V, I swapped out the magnetic WHITAKER WOODWORKING sign on the door for one that read HOME & HEARTH REALTY. Yep, I wore two hats. The hard hat when moonlighting as a carpenter for my uncle, and a metaphorical second hat when working my day job as a property manager for a real estate business. This morning, I sported the metaphorical hat as I headed up Hillsboro Pike into Nashville. Fifteen minutes later, I turned onto Sweetbriar Avenue. In the driveway of the house on the corner sat a shiny midnight blue Infiniti Q70L sedan with vanity plates that read TGENTRY. My shackles rose at the sight.

Thaddeus Gentry III owned Gentry Real Estate Development, Inc. or, as I called it, GREED Incorporated. Okay, so I'd added an extra E to make the spelling work. Still, it was true. The guy was as money-hungry and ruthless as they come. He was singlehandedly responsible for the gentrification of several old Nashville neighborhoods. While gentrification wasn't necessarily a bad thing—after all it rid the city of ramshackle houses in dire need of repairs—Thad Gentry took advantage of homeowners, offering them pennies on the dollar, knowing they couldn't afford the increase in property taxes that would result as their modest neighborhoods transformed into upscale communities. He'd harass holdouts by reporting any city code violations, no matter how minor. He also formed homeowners' associations in the newly renovated neighborhoods, and ensured the HOA put pressure on the remaining original residents to bring their houses up to snuff. These unfortunate folks found they no longer felt at home and usually gave in and moved on . . . to where, who knows?

When I'd come by a week ago in a final attempt to collect from the tenants, I'd noticed a for sale sign in the yard where Thad Gentry's car was parked. The sign was gone now. *Had Gentry bought the property? Had he set his sights on the neighborhood?*

Paw Enforcement - Excerpt

Chapter One

Job Insecurity

Fort Worth Police Officer Megan Luz

My rusty-haired partner lay convulsing on the hot asphalt, his jaw clenching and his body involuntarily curling into a jittery fetal position as two probes delivered 1,500 volts of electricity to his groin. The crotch of his police-issue trousers darkened as he lost control of his bladder.

I'd never felt close to my partner in the six months we'd worked together, but at that particular moment I sensed a strong bond. The connection likely stemmed from the fact that we were indeed connected then--by the two wires leading from the Taser in my hand to my partner's twitching testicles.

#

I didn't set out to become a hero. I decided on a career in law enforcement for three other reasons:

1) Having been a twirler in my high school's marching band, I knew how to handle a baton.

2) Other than barking short orders or rattling off Miranda rights, working as a police officer wouldn't require me to talk much.

3) I had an excess of pent-up anger. Might as well put it to good use, right?

Of course I didn't plan to be a street cop forever. Just long enough to work my way up to detective. A lofty goal, but I knew I could do it-- even if nobody else did.

I'd enjoyed my studies in criminal justice at Sam Houston State University in Hunstville, Texas, especially the courses in criminal psychology. No, I'm not some sick, twisted creep who gets off on hearing about criminals who steal, rape, and murder. I just thought that if we could figure out why criminals do bad things, maybe we could stop them, you know?

To supplement my student loans, I'd worked part-time at the gift shop in the nearby state prison museum, selling tourists such quality souvenirs as ceramic ash trays made by the prisoners or decks of cards containing prison trivia. The unit had once been home to Clyde Barrow of Bonnie and Clyde fame and was also the site of an eleven-day siege in 1974 spearheaded by heroin kingpin Fredrick Gomez Carrasco, jailed for killing a police officer. Our top-selling item was a child's time-out chair fashioned after Old Sparky, the last remaining electric chair used in Texas. Talk about cruel and unusual punishment.

To the corner, little Billy.

No, Mommy, no! Anything but the chair!

I'd looked forward to becoming a cop, keeping the streets safe for citizens, maintaining law and order, promoting civility and justice. Such noble ideals, right?

What I hadn't counted on was that I'd be working with a force full of macho shitheads. With my uncanny luck, I'd been assigned to partner with the most macho, most shit-headed cop of all, Derek the "Big Dick" Mackey. As implied in the aforementioned reference to twitching testicles, our partnership had not ended well.

That's why I was sitting here outside the chief's office in a cheap plastic chair, chewing my thumbnail down to a painful nub, waiting to find out whether I still had a job. Evidently, Tasering your partner in the *cojones* is considered not only an overreaction, but also a blatant violation of department policy, one which carried the potential penalty of dismissal from the force, not to mention a criminal assault charge.

So much for those noble ideals, huh?

I ran a finger over my upper lip, blotting the nervous sweat that had formed there. Would I be booted off the force after only six months on duty?

With the city's budget crisis, there'd been threats of cutbacks and layoffs across the board. No department would be spared. If the chief had to fire anyone, he'd surely start with the rookie with the Irish temper. If the chief canned me, what would I do? My aspirations of becoming a detective would go down the toilet. Once again I'd be Megan Luz, a.k.a. "The Loser." As you've probably guessed, my pent-up anger had a lot to do with that nickname.

I pulled my telescoping baton from my belt and flicked my wrist to extend it. *Snap!* Though my police baton had a different feel from the twirling baton I'd used in high school, I'd quickly learned that with a few minor adjustments to accommodate the distinctive weight distribution I could perform many of the same tricks with it. I began to work the stick, performing a basic flat spin. The repetitive motion calmed me, helped me think. It was like a twirling metal stress ball. *Swish-swish-swish.*

The chief's door opened and three men exited. All wore navy tees emblazoned with white letters spelling BOMB SQUAD stretched tight across well-developed pecs. Though the bomb squad was officially part of the Fort Worth Fire Department, the members worked closely with the police. Where there's a bomb, there's a crime, after all. Most likely these men were here to discuss safety procedures for the upcoming Concerts in the Park. After what happened at the Boston marathon, extra precautions were warranted for large public events.

The guy in front, a blond with a military-style haircut, cut his eyes my way. He watched me spin my baton for a moment, then dipped his head in acknowledgement when my gaze met his. He issued the standard southern salutation. "Hey."

His voice was deep with a subtle rumble, like far-off thunder warning of an oncoming storm. The guy wasn't tall, but he was broad-shouldered, muscular, and undeniably masculine. He had dark green eyes and a dimple in his chin that drew my eyes downward, over his soft, sexy mouth, and back up again.

A hot flush exploded through me. I tried to nod back at him, but my muscles seemed to have atrophied. My hand stopped moving and clutched my baton in a death grip. All I could do was watch as he and the other men continued into the hall and out of sight.

Blurgh. Acting like a frigid virgin. How humiliating!

Once the embarrassment waned, I began to wonder. Had the bomb squad guy found me attractive? Is that why he'd greeted me? Or was he simply being friendly to a fellow public servant?

My black locks were pulled back in a tight, torturous bun, a style that enabled me to look professional on the force while allowing me to retain my feminine allure after hours. There were only so many sacrifices I was willing to make for employment and my long, lustrous hair was not one of them. My freckles showed through my light makeup. Hard to feel like a tough cop if you're wearing too much foundation or more than one coat of mascara. Fortunately, I had enough natural coloring to get by with little in the way of cosmetics. I was a part Irish-American, part Mexican-American mutt, with just enough Cherokee blood to give me an instinctive urge to dance in the rain but not enough to qualify me for any college scholarships. My figure was neither thin nor voluptuous, but my healthy diet and regular exercise kept me in decent shape. It was entirely possible that the guy had been checking me out. Right?

I mentally chastised myself. *Chill, Megan.* I hadn't had a date since I'd joined the force, but so what? I had more important things to deal with at the moment. I collapsed my baton, returned it to my belt, and took a deep breath to calm my nerves.

The chief's secretary, a middle-aged brunette wearing a poly-blend dress, sat at her desk typing a report into the computer. She had twice as much butt as chair, her thighs draping over the sides of the seat. But who could blame her? Judging from the photos on her desk, she'd squeezed out three children in rapid succession. Having grown up in a family of five kids, I knew mothers had little time to devote to themselves when their kids were young and constantly needed mommy to feed them, clean up their messes, and bandage their various boo-boos. She wore no jewelry, no makeup, and no nail polish. The chief deserved credit for not hiring a younger, prettier, better accessorized woman for the job. Obviously, she'd been hired for her mad office skills. She'd handled a half dozen phone calls in the short time I'd been waiting and her fingers moved over the keyboard at such a speedy pace it was a miracle her hands didn't burst into flame. Whatever she was being paid, it wasn't enough.

The woman's phone buzzed again and she punched her intercom button. "Yessir?" She paused a moment. "I'll send her in." She hung up the phone and turned to me. "The chief is ready for you."

"Thanks." I stood on wobbly legs.

Would the chief take my badge today? Was my career in law enforcement over?

Death, Taxes, and a French Manicure - Excerpt

Chapter One

Some People Just Need Shooting

When I was nine, I formed a Silly Putty pecker for my Ken doll, knowing he'd have no chance of fulfilling Barbie's needs given the permanent state of erectile dysfunction with which the toy designers at Mattel had cursed him. I knew a little more about sex than most girls, what with growing up in the country and all. The first time I saw our neighbor's Black Angus bull mount an unsuspecting heifer, my two older brothers explained it all to me.

"He's getting him some," they'd said.

"Some what?" I'd asked.

"Nookie."

We watched through the barbed wire fence until the strange ordeal was over. Frankly, the process looked somewhat uncomfortable for the cow, who continued to chew her cud throughout the entire encounter. But when the bull dismounted, nuzzled her chin, and wandered away, I swore I saw a smile on that cow's face and a look of quiet contentment in her eyes. She was in love.

I'd been in search of that same feeling for myself ever since.

My partner and I had spent the afternoon huddled at a cluttered desk in the back office of an auto parts store perusing the owner's financial records, searching for evidence of tax fraud. Yeah, you got me. I work for the IRS. Not exactly the kind of career that makes a person popular at cocktail parties. But those brave enough to get to know me learn I'm actually a nice person, fun even, and they have nothing to fear. I have better things to do than nickel and dime taxpayers whose worst crime was inflating the value of the Glen Campbell albums they donated to Goodwill.

"I'll be right back, Tara." My partner smoothed the front of his starched white button-down as he stood from the folding chair. Eddie Bardin was tall, lean, and African-American, but having been raised in the upper-middle-class, predominately white Dallas suburbs, he had a hard time connecting to his roots. He'd had nothing to overcome, unless you counted his affinity for Phil Collins' music, Heineken beer, and khaki chinos, tastes which he had yet to conquer. Eddie was more L.L. Bean than L.L. Cool J.

I nodded to Eddie and tucked an errant strand of my chestnut hair behind my ear. Turning back to the spreadsheet in front of me, I flicked aside the greasy burger and onion ring wrappers the store's owner, Jack Battaglia, had left on the desk after lunch. I couldn't make heads or tails out of the numbers on the page. Battaglia didn't know jack about keeping books and, judging from his puny salaries account, he'd been too cheap to hire a professional.

A few seconds after Eddie left the room, the door to the office banged open. Battaglia loomed in the doorway, his husky body filling the narrow space. He wore a look of purpose and his store's trademark bright green jumpsuit, the cheerful color at odds with the open box cutter clutched in his furry-knuckled fist.

"Hey!" Instinctively, I leapt from my seat, the metal chair falling over behind me and clanging to the floor.

Battaglia lunged at me. My heart whirled in my chest. There was no time to pull my gun. The best I could do was throw out my right arm to deflect his attempt to plunge the blade into my jugular. The sharp blade slid across my forearm, just above my wrist, but with so much adrenaline rocketing through my system, I felt no immediate pain. If not for the blood seeping through the sleeve of my navy nylon raid jacket, I wouldn't have even known I'd been cut. Underneath was my favorite pink silk blouse, a coup of a find on the clearance rack at Neiman Marcus Last Call, now sliced open, the blood-soaked material gaping to reveal a short but deep gash.

My jaw clamped tighter than a chastity belt on a pubescent princess. This jerk was going down.

My block had knocked him to the side. Taking advantage of our relative positioning, I threw a roundhouse kick to Battaglia's stomach, my steel-toed cherry-red Doc Martens sinking into his soft paunch. The shoes were the perfect combination of utility and style, another great find at a two-for-one sale at the Galleria.

The kick didn't take the beer-bellied bastard out of commission, but at least it sent him backwards a few feet, putting a little more distance between us. A look of surprise flashed across Battaglia's face as he stumbled backward. He clearly hadn't expected a skinny, five-foot-two-inch bookish woman to put up such a fierce fight.

Neener-neener.

Love, Luck, and Little Green Men - Excerpt

CHAPTER ONE - MONDAY, FEBRUARY 14TH
MIXED BOUQUETS, MIXED MESSAGES

Another Valentine's Day and here I was again. Lonely. Loveless. Lover-less.
Yep, I'm unlucky in love. Unlucky in just about everything else, too. Life tried, and time again, to kick my ass. But, you know what? Life could piss off. I, Erin Flaherty, would not go down without a fight.

***

For the third time in as many months, I sat at the counter of my shoe repair shop screwing a new tap on the heel of a men's size thirteen tap shoe. Part of me wanted to scold my son for abusing his dance shoes, but another part knew the broken tap was a sign of his passion for dance. With his enormous feet, athletic style, and unbridled enthusiasm, Riley could stomp a stage into splinters. Heck, I'd broken a tap or two myself over the years. Might as well cut the kid some slack.

My shop wasn't much to brag about, just a small foyer and stockroom with walls painted a soft sage green and dark wood floors that, judging from the multitude of scars, were likely original. Two wooden chairs flanked the front door. Not that I was ever so busy customers needed a place to sit while they waited their turn, but best to be prepared just in case, right? A brass coat tree nestled in one corner, an oval standing mirror in the other. The white Formica countertop supported an outdated but functional cash register and one of the world's last remaining black-and-white portable TV's. A full-color map of County Cork, Ireland and a poster of Saint Fin Barre's Cathedral, a County Cork historical landmark, graced the walls, giving the shop a touch of Irish kitsch.

The bells hanging from the front door tinkled and a blast of brisk winter wind blew into my shop, carrying a sweet, flowery scent with it. I looked up to see an enormous bouquet of long-stem roses, six red and six yellow, making its way inside. My heart performed a pirouette in my chest and I emitted an involuntary squeal. "Flowers? For me?"

Dumb question, really. I was the only one in the shop. But you can't blame me for being surprised. The last time anyone had given me flowers was when Riley's father had shown up in the delivery room with a tiny bouquet of carnations and an even tinier engagement ring. That was fourteen years—and what seemed like a lifetime—ago. I'd kept the flowers but refused the ring. The right choice, obviously, given the look of relief on Matthew's face when I'd handed the small velvet-covered box back to him. But who could blame him? Like me, he'd been only nineteen, much too young to deal with a new baby and a wife, though not too young to knock me up, the knucklehead. He'd promised to pull out. Never trust a guy with a hard on.

Of course it takes two to tango, and I've accepted my share of the blame. Or should I say credit? When I think of my son, of what a clever and caring kid he's turned out to be, it's impossible to consider him as a mistake.

The roses made their way toward me, bringing their lovely smell along with them, coming to rest on the countertop next to the cash register. Their courier stepped aside to reveal himself. I knew the face in an instant. Strong-jawed, with the ruddy complexion of a man who'd spent a decade toiling at the dockyards of Dublin. Dark hair worn closely cropped in a no-fuss style. Intelligent, soulful eyes under thick brows. The roguish smile that revealed an upper bicuspid chipped in a life-changing moment the tooth would never let him forget.

Brendan.

"Happy Saint Valentine's Day, Erin."

Would I ever tire of that deep Irish brogue?

59284331R00075